DATE DUE		

FINAL SEASON

WAYNE ARTHURSON

THISTLEDOWN PRESS

National Library of Canada Cataloguing in Publication Data

Arthurson, Wayne, 1962–
Final season

ISBN 1-894345-48-7
I. Native peoples—Manitoba—Fiction.* I. Title.
PS8551.R888F56 2002   C813'.6   C2002-910961-2
PR9199.4.A77F56 2002

Cover photograph by Janey Foster/Masterfile
Cover and book design by Jackie Forrie
Typeset by Thistledown Press Ltd.
Printed and bound in Canada

Lyrics to "The Dead Heart" by Midnight Oil
Used with permission

Thistledown Press Ltd.
633 Main Street
Saskatoon, Saskatchewan
S7H 0J8

Thistledown Press gratefully acknowledges the financial assis-
tance of the Canada Council for the Arts, the Saskatchewan Arts
Board, and the Government of Canada through the Book
Publishing Industry Development Program for its publishing
program.

ACKNOWLEDGEMENTS

Thank you to: my aunts, uncles, cousins and the residents of Norway House and Grand Rapids for their hospitality and stories; my mother whose strength has always been an inspiration and my father who invited me on the trip that inspired this book; my sisters; all the bands who allowed me to backstop their musical efforts; Doug Willy for introducing me to the world of IBAs; Dr. Gavin Hanke for info on fish and stuff in Lake Winnipeg; that unidentified employee of the Manitoba Legislature archives who faxed me various pieces of information that I forgot to pay for (sorry); *AlbertaViews* and the CBC for using parts of this novel; Lorraine Lafranchise for the use of the laptop; Allison, Audrey, Carol, David, Lorraine, Pam, Robin and Tom (my writing group); Dave Johnston and *Vue Weekly*; David Arnason for the edit; and anybody else who read my stuff, gave me work, fed me, bought me beer and/or supported me.

Finally, infinite thanks must go to my wife Auni. Everything I have accomplished in the past ten years is because of her.

Although the towns of Grand Rapids and Norway House actually exist, this is a work of fiction and should not be confused as historically and geographically accurate. Everything in this book is the product of the author's imagination, unless I say different.

To Auni, who taught me that love is the true meaning of life.

We carry in our hearts the true country
and that cannot be stolen
We follow in the steps of our ancestry
and that cannot be broken.

— "The Dead Heart", Midnight Oil

TWO YEARS AGO

They carried the body in a blanket, using the four corners as handles. The body was heavy and Albert and Fency's boy adjusted their grip every few seconds to prevent dropping it. And every time they did this, the body bounced and made the blanket seem even heavier.

Albert Apetagon was at the back end of the blanket and his position forced him to look down on the body. The light from the stars and the half moon gave the gray skin a pale glow. Albert tried to look forward at the boy's back, but every time the blanket slipped, he had to look down to adjust. Albert knew Fency's boy had the awkward position of carrying the blanket with his hands behind his back, but he also knew it was better to have him at the front so he didn't have to look at the body. Bringing him along on this project was one thing, asking him to constantly look down on his father's body while he was carrying it was something else. It was difficult enough for Albert. Barry Fency had been his friend since those years on the Keweetan, but he couldn't subject the man's son to stare down at him as they carried him to the lake.

The constant jerking of the body and the shifting of the weight drove sharp biting pains into Albert's arms, back and shoulders and he considered asking the boy to stop and rest for a few minutes, but then dismissed the idea. They had to get the body out to the boat and then out to the lake before anybody realized it was gone. And Albert knew if they stopped for even a second, it would give them time to think about what they were doing, and they might change their minds. Even now Albert was questioning his motives.

GRAND RAPIDS

1

Albert Apetagon shut off his single 35 h.p. engine and let the boat drift in. The bottom of the boat scraped against the rough sand and Albert leaned back against the warm engine, forcing the bow up so that the boat would slide further up the shore. The wake from his engine gave the boat another small push to the beach and then it stopped, padding gently against the makeshift dock. The dock wasn't anything special, just five wooden pallets lashed together with some twine; not something you could walk on, but it kept the boat from drifting onto the lake during the night. Albert had staked one end of the pallets to the ground with some tenting pegs and allowed the other end to float gently in the water. He got to his feet by pushing against the engine for leverage and slowly climbed through the middle of the boat, over his nets and the four remaining fish cartons. He grabbed the front line and quickly stepped over the bow end and onto the shore. The boat rocked back and forth and began to drift in the wake from the shore, but Albert held onto the line and pulled it back in. He grabbed the bow, lifted the front end of the boat and dragged it further ashore. Even though the broadness of his shoulders had drifted to his waist in the past bunch of years, most of his strength remained. Lifting and dragging his one-ton, three-seater aluminum Lund with a 35 horsepower Evinrude was a relatively easy task for the fisherman. A difficult task was lifting 25 cartons full of whitefish up to the selling dock, especially when Hydro shut down the spillways of the dam upstream on the Saskatchewan River, which they usually did during fishing season. Hydro's shutdown of the spillways dropped the level of the river by a couple of meters, so a small boat like Albert's would bounce against the pilings of Barings' dock, instead of against the dock itself. That meant he had to lift full cartons of fish — something like 35 pounds — from the bottom of the boat and up over his head to reach the selling dock. Barings, the fish company buyer, wouldn't lift a finger to help; he'd just stand at the edge of the dock, his feet always right at the spot where you'd be aiming to set down a carton of fish.

"Looks like a pretty good load today, Albert," Barings would say if he had more than seven or eight loads to lift up. If Albert had less, he'd say, "Looks like a pretty slow load today, Albert."

And that's all he'd say about the fish. He wouldn't say how much they'd fetch, what the daily price was for whitefish, suckers or whatever the company was looking for, or how much the company was going to pay you for your catch. All that information was written down on the company tally sheet that Barings carried on his clipboard and then tore off and handed to the fishermen when the weighing was done. In fact, there was no need for Barings to hang around the dock while they unloaded the cartons. He knew the fish still had to be gutted and cleaned, the heads and entrails chucked to the gulls and pelicans, before getting them weighed, but he always hung around at the dock while someone unloaded their fish. He'd fill the air with mindless chatter: the weather, the colour of the lake, Hydro's new project up at Swan Lake, whatever. And it always took Barings a second or two to realize that he was in your way.

"You know, Charlie at the school board says they're looking for a buncha guys once they get government approval for the new project and I was thinking once the season ends, that would be it for me. I'm getting sick of this temporary shit, three months here and there. That new Hydro project is at least five years steady work or more, just like the dam in the 60s, and for two old guys like us . . . oh, sorry Albert, let me get out of your way . . . I figure it's just the right amount of time and then we can grab a pension and retire."

Solomon Jacks once said it was the company that was responsible for what had happened to Barings. Barings was once like the rest of them, a fisherman who spent the day out on the lake in his Lund boat, lying out the lines, pulling in piles of fish and storing them in those styrofoam coolers that anybody could get at the Northern store. But a few years ago, Barings sold both his boat (engines and equipment included) and his license to the company. After a week of orientation in Winnipeg, Barings became the buyer for the northwest coast of the lake.

"It was that week of orientation that did him in," Sol explained. "It happens every time you become an employee of a big corporation, they have to orientate you. Sometimes it's an afternoon and sometimes it's a couple of weeks or so. Christ knows what the hell they can orient about for a week or two but whatever they do, the result is always the same. It's like they take the smart part of your brain away or they shrink it or something and you forget almost everything you did before. The only thing your brain is capable of working on is breathing, eating, shitting and anything related to the company. Anything else doesn't calculate anymore."

"Where the hell did that come from?" Albert asked Sol.

"Doesn't it make sense to you?" Sol asked in return.

"When you explain it the way you do, it seems to make sense," Albert said, "but I'm just wondering where that idea came from. Did it just pop into your head or have you been thinking about this for a long time? Sounds like you've been thinking about it for awhile."

Sol's face went red with embarrassment. "So I thought about it for awhile. So what? Is there something wrong with thinking? Did you ever wonder why or how Barings became the way he is now?"

"Nope," Albert said with a shake of his head. "Barings has always been the way he is now. He was like that when he took over on the Keweetan after Jerry Harrison died, or so Barry Fency and your brother Abe used to say. That's one of the main reasons why Abe doesn't like him that much, because of the time they worked on the Keweetan. And Barings was like that when he was a supervisor on the dam. It's just that we've been used to him on the lake, that for a while we forgot what he was really like. I'm just surprised that you've been thinking about it for such a long time."

"I haven't been thinking about it for a long time. I've just been thinking about it off and on for a long time. There's a difference."

Albert nodded. "Give you that but don't know why you'd want to spend a lot of time thinking about Barings and his job as a buyer for the company."

Sol laughed loudly. It was an infectious happy sound, like a kid laughing, and Albert had no choice but to smile, even though he had no idea what Sol was laughing about. "You'd be surprised about the things I think about, Albert. Very surprised," said Sol. "I think very differently than the average person."

"I don't doubt that."

"No, I'm serious. I look at things quite differently from you or anybody else," Sol said in a serious tone. "And I can prove it."

"Since I've got nothing better to do with my time, Sol, I'm going to keep on listening. But not for long."

"Okay. This is why I think differently than you," Sol started. "If you wanted to pick up a woman in this town Albert, a good-looking woman mind you, not just any woman, where would you go?"

"Now that's thinking different Sol, asking me where I would go to pick up women," Albert laughed. "I don't think Elaine would much like me doing that."

"Forget Elaine," Sol said, but then quickly changed his mind. "No forget I said that. Just pretend you're somebody else, like say . . . Fency's boy. Where would he go to meet a woman?"

"Fency's like me. He's already got somebody with Keung's daughter. He'd be fucking insane if he tried to pick up some other woman. She's the best thing that ever happened to him, and he knows it, too, even though he doesn't like to admit it. If it wasn't for Julie, our young Fency would be lost. She may be young but she gives him a base. With me, it's Elaine. For Fency, it's Julie Keung. She's something he can tie his life to. If she wasn't here, he'd have left after his dad died. Fency's not a stupid boy anymore. He knows what's important and he's not going to ruin it by chasing after other women. Besides, Keung would kill him if Fency broke his daughter's heart by chasing after other women, we both know that."

"Oh, forget Fency then," Sol said in exasperation. "Just pretend, will ya Albert. You know the town, you know how things work. Where would a single guy go to pick up women in this town?"

"I don't know. Pinky's, I guess?"

"That's right!" Sol said, snapping his fingers. "Pinky's! That's the right answer. Everybody would agree if you wanted to meet women in this shit town, that's the place you'd want to go. And that's where everybody goes. But in my head, that's the worst place in town to meet women."

"It is?"

"No shit it is. What kind of women are you going to meet in Pinky's anyways?"

"I don't know, I've been a married man for over 30 years. I didn't know shit about picking up women before I got married so I'm sure as shit I know nothing about picking up women now."

"So do most guys in this town. So do most guys," Sol said, waving his finger like some type of old-fashioned schoolteacher. "Only good ole Sol knows."

"Okay Sol. Where is the best place in town to pick up women?"

Sol waved his hand in the air. "No, no, no. It's not that easy Albert. First I have to tell you why Pinky's is the worst place in town to pick up women."

"Jeez, Sol. How long is this thing going to take? Sometime this year the fishing season is going to start up again and I'm going to have get back out on the lake."

"You're the one who wanted to know how I think different."

"No. You're the one who started this thing by insisting that he thinks different and wanted, for some fucking reason, to prove to me he thinks different. Let's get this over with by telling you that I believe you Sol. I believe that you think different. You've proven to me that you think differently by starting this whole stupid thing in the first place."

"Sorry Albert. It's like you've dropped your lines into the biggest school of fish in the lake and you're starting to pull them in fully loaded: once it gets started, there's nothing you can do to stop it. I'm like that fishing line right now, you got to pull it all in."

"Sometimes you've pulled in enough fish and if you don't stop, you're going to miss the weighing deadline." With two fingers, Albert pantomimed snipping a fishing line. "Better hang on Sol, 'cause I'm cutting you loose."

Solomon Jacks never got the chance that day to finish his theory, but Albert knew that one day, when he was feeling generous or when Sol had him cornered, the picking up women theory would come up again. That's the way Sol was, he didn't like to leave important things, like a theory on how the world worked, unfinished. Albert knew Sol thought different, the man had proved it by espousing his theory on why Barings was the way he was, now that he was the company buyer. Sol was the only person who could come up with such a theory, and though Albert knew he was mostly kidding, he knew there was a little bit of truth in Sol's words about Barings and the company's orientation.

Before he took the job as the company buyer, Barings had been a fisherman on the lake longer than anyone, including the Jacks boys, Sol and Abe. And when Albert returned to fishing after his time with Hydro on the dam project, it was Barings who helped him out, who showed him where to find fish, who reminded him to watch for circling pelicans or the changing colours of the lake. And it was Barings who retaught him the trick of looking up at the clouds to see any reflections from the lake and any changes of colour up there. You couldn't do it all the time, only when thick and grey clouds covered the sky and hung low over your head like a wall threatening to fall. The clouds would weigh you down and make you feel like someone was staring over your shoulders all day. When the sky was like that, you had to keep forcing yourself to sit up straight and stretch your back or you'd get a real nasty crick in your neck and shoulders from hunching over all the time. If you knew to watch the reflection of the lake on the low clouds and look for any movement in the colour, you could find a lot of fish. But since he'd become the company buyer, Barings seemed to have forgotten anything about fishing and if you'd just met him, you'd never guess he'd spent more than 25 years on the lake. And you'd never guess that it was

Barings' trick that Albert used on one of those heavy cloudy days to catch his biggest load ever — 25 cartons of fish.

Lifting those 25 cartons made his shoulders feel like mush and if it wasn't for the Jacks boys and Tom Simpson and Barry Fency's boy hanging around after weighing their catches, and helping him out with the cleaning and gutting, he would have never gotten his load weighed and sold in time for the deadline. But that was how it worked sometimes. If someone was late coming in because of the weather, or if they had a big catch, some guys would hang around and help you clean them so Barings could get them weighed and sold before the day was over. Usually it was the older fishermen who helped and Fency's boy. He wasn't like the other younger fishermen because he wasn't a hired hand for Barings' company. He had inherited his boat and license two years ago, after the death of his father.

But it didn't matter how many cartons of fish you caught that day — a hundred or a thousand — if the sales deadline of 3 p.m. passed and you still hadn't been weighed, every bit of your catch was just food for the gulls and pelicans. Barings would never give any leeway because "company rules are company rules and if I give you guys one minute one day, it's two minutes the next and soon I'm sitting out here at five o'clock weighing fish for you guys."

But two years ago, not long after he registered his biggest catch ever, Albert asked Barings if he could borrow the company boat for a few hours one night. And Barings didn't flat out refuse him. He listened to

Albert's reasons for wanting to borrow it and then thought about it for a few seconds.

"You really serious about this Albert?" Barings asked.

"Very serious."

"You could get in a lot of trouble."

"What are they going to do to me? I'm just an old fisherman. Nothing going to happen to me that I can't handle."

"What about Elaine? You talk to her about this?"

"Yeah. I talked to her."

"What she say?"

"She's not happy about it, but she knows nothing's going to stop me. She's resigned herself to pretending I'm just going to do some late night fishing."

"Yeah, but this isn't some lark. You're not just going out in the middle night to drink a few beers or to check out the stars."

"I know what I'm going to do. You going to lend me the boat?"

"I'm not sure, that's a big thing to ask," Barings said. He went silent for a few minutes, thinking. "Who else is in on this?"

"I'd rather not say. The less you know the better."

"If I'm going to lend you the company boat so you can do this, I want to know everything. I'll be risking my job here."

"If you think your job is so goddamn important then forget it," Albert said angrily.

Barings snapped back. "Don't pull that shit on me, Albert. I know you guys go back a long way but remember, we worked on the Keweetan for two years before you came along. This is just as hard for me as it is for you."

"Then you gonna help us or what?"

"I want to know who else is in on it."

Albert thought for a half a minute and then told him. "There's Sol."

Barings nodded. "Figured. Abe too?"

Albert shook his head. "We asked him, but he said no. He expects us to get in big trouble."

"You probably will," Barings said. "Anybody else?"

Albert looked at Barings and then after a second said, "His boy."

"You're bringing him on this?"

"We didn't invite him, but when he found out, he demanded to be a part of it."

"That's not a good idea. You, me and Sol, that's okay, we're just some old fishermen, but he's young. Just got his life back on track after the fire. He can't get mixed up in this."

"I tried to tell him no, but he wouldn't take no for an answer. It is his old man we're talking about, so he does have a right."

Barings sighed deeply. "This is getting crazy. We're talking big trouble here."

Albert nodded. "I know, but it's got to be done."

"Not really it doesn't. We can just forget it."

"That's a load of crap and you know it," Albert barked.

Barings nodded, and for several days refused to talk about the subject. But in the end, he did finally let Albert use the boat. Even though he was the company buyer, he still was an old fisherman. And old fishermen on the lake always helped out other old fishermen. And sometimes even a few of the young fishermen helped out too.

So the day Albert caught 25 cartons worth of fish, the Jacks boys, Tom Simpson and Fency stayed two hours later than they would've had to and helped Albert clean and sell his load. Albert appreciated it, but except for a simple thanks to each of them, he didn't make any special note of it. He'd done it for them and others before and would probably do it again. There was no need to make a special deal about it.

But today, there had only been four and a half cartons. Even so, lifting them up to the dock while Barings rambled about the new Hydro project and then pulling the fish out of the icy water in the cartons and repeating the same movement over and over again to clean and gut them, made the arthritis in Albert's hands and shoulders start to tingle. Once he finished and got his invoice from Barings, he climbed back into his boat and motored over to his makeshift dock on a little secluded beach about half a kilometre north of the mouth of the river. Albert tied the boat line to one of the tent pegs and stood at attention so he could do the shoulder exercises he was supposed to do when his arthritis started to act up. He lifted both arms, from the side of his waist, up over his head. He was supposed to do twenty, but he stopped at ten. The next set was the same type of exercise but the arms came forward and then over his head. Again, he stopped at ten and started on the third set, lifting the arms behind his back as far as he could. He paused briefly at the fifth one and was going to stop there, but a voice called out to him.

"Aren't you supposed to do twenty of those?" the voice said. "I remember Elaine saying that you were told to do twenty of each, but I only counted ten and you've only done five in the back."

Albert recognized the voice of Sol Jacks, the younger of the two Jack brothers. Albert dropped his arms, rubbed his shoulders and turned to face Sol. "My arms hurt when I do twenty. Ten's enough."

Sol laughed. At barely five and half feet tall, he was almost a foot shorter than Albert. Like Albert though, Sol's face was weathered and wrinkled like an old wallet, and he constantly squinted, the result of spending hours on the lake without the help of sunglasses. Only the younger fishermen wore sunglasses. Albert, the two Jacks brothers and a few others couldn't be bothered; sunglasses took away all the depth and made the shifting colours of the lake — signs pointing to or away from a school of fish — difficult to spot. The younger fishermen had all the electronic and expensive equipment — depth gauges, fish sonars, and the like — so they didn't need to rely on the shifting shades of blue on the lake. Of course that didn't mean they caught any more fish than Albert and the Jacks brothers, just that they could wear sunglasses on the lake.

"Your arms hurt 'cause you don't do the exercises the way you're supposed to," Sol said. "If they say you gotta do twenty, then you gotta do twenty."

Albert shook his head. "When did you become so concerned for my welfare, Sol?"

"Not your welfare, Albert, I just don't feel like fishing alone out there. Too many young guys with their fancy gear out there and not enough of us old-timers."

"You always have your brother."

Sol spit on the beach. "Might as well be fishing alone. Abe doesn't like sharing, you know that. Likes to hang out by himself. You get within a mile or two of him and he'll move, even if he found the biggest spot in the lake. He'll move and make you think he was dragging in crap instead of fish."

"And then when you leave," Albert added with a quick laugh, "he'd come back to the spot and suck up all the fish. 'Course with the company boys, all of us would do that."

"No doubt, but we independent guys got to stick together. You gotta help out a bit, share some of the fish, but Abe just doesn't get it. If another guy goes down, Barings will just snap up his license and his boat and send out one of his boys."

"In five years, though, it'll just be Barings and his boys out there. Guys like you and me getting too old for this."

"I'm not old."

"Yeah, but I am," Albert said. "My hands and shoulders hurting so much sometimes in the cold, it's getting difficult hauling in the net."

Sol laughed and slapped Albert on the back. "That's why you gotta do the exercises the way they tell you. So you can keep going for the next five years."

"Ha! Five years! I'll barely last next season." Sol opened his mouth to say something but Albert waved him quiet. "Don't worry Sol. It's just old age. My body can't take it anymore. Time to move on and try something more relaxing anyway."

"You can't relax, Albert," Sol said with a smile. "You and Elaine work too hard to relax."

"Going to have to though. My body can't take it anymore." Albert put an arm around Sol's shoulders and steered him away from the beach. "Come on, Sol, give me a ride so I don't have to walk all the way into town."

"Where's your truck?"

"Truck fucked up this morning."

"Again! You've got to get yourself a new truck."

"With what? Fish? There's not enough fish in that lake anymore. I could fish all year and still wouldn't make enough money to buy a used truck, let alone a new one."

"Hydro says they're thinking of upping the stock for the lake this year."

"Says who?"

"Jesus, Albert. Where the hell do you think I've been these last few days? Sleeping in? Christ, when I tell you that Hydro's thinking about upping the stock for this year, it means that Hydro told me that."

"Well, Hydro's been saying that for a couple years."

"Take it from me," Sol said, "this year is the one."

"Sounds then like you guys got the IBA all signed up."

"We made a deal," Sol said. "A really good one, too. Probably enough retro money out front so you can get a new truck."

"I'm going to need a treaty number to get in on that," Albert said.

"So get yourself a treaty number! You'd have no problem. I could probably get it backdated for you too."

Albert shrugged noncommittally. "I don't know. Seems like a lot of hassle."

"For you, with all your connections, it'd be easy as pie. And with the IBA kicking in, you not only get enough to buy a new truck, you could probably get a new boat."

"I don't think I'm going to need a new boat."

Sol quietly looked at Albert for several seconds before speaking. "You really thinking of quitting the lake?"

"Yep. Figured this might be my last day. But don't tell anyone. Only you and Elaine know about this."

"They'll get nothing out of me." The two men separated, Sol to the driver's side of the truck and Albert to the passenger. Sol opened his door but didn't climb in. "What about your boat and license? Any of your boys interested?"

Albert shook his head. "Not one. Larry's got a good job with Hydro at Split Lake, Frank's got six more years till his army pension kicks in, last I heard Benny was working rigs near Fort McMurray, and shit, Paul, he keeps getting so many cheques from you guys in the band that he couldn't be bothered."

"Hey don't knock the band, we take care of our own."

"A little too much care if you ask me," Albert said. "Sometimes you gotta cut your losses, especially if they don't even live here, like Paul."

Sol tapped his finger against the hood of the truck. "Some people take longer than others to clean up. They gotta want it and right now Paul doesn't seem ready. But one day, Vancouver will have nothing for him anymore. But we can't cut him loose. Just imagine what would have happened if we cut our losses with Jessica, then where would we be, eh Albert? Getting Jessica clean and back on her feet wasn't easy, but now she's one of the chief negotiators for the band and she takes good care of her kids. I'll tell you something Albert, if it wasn't for Jessica, we wouldn't have gotten the IBA that we just got from Hydro. She's one hell of a woman and you should be proud of her."

"I'm proud of her," Albert said, rubbing his neck. "Reminds me a lot of her mother. And she's got a bunch of good kids too. But her oldest boy, David, don't know. He could go either way."

"Kids are like that. You were probably like that, I'm guessing."

"Yeah, well, I got lucky. I got a job on the Keweetan and got out of Norway House."

"Then maybe David will get lucky," Sol said, climbing in the truck. Albert climbed into the passenger side. "Say how old is David anyway? Fifteen right?" Sol asked.

"Thirteen," Albert said shaking his head. "Why'd you ask?"

"Well if he was fifteen he could have taken over your license next year when he turned sixteen. He's got a treaty number as well so he'd get more out of the season. That is, if he liked fishing. You ever take him on the lake?"

"When they were little that's all they wanted to do. But not as much now. Last year was the last time, I think," Albert said.

"Did he like it?"

Albert shrugged. "Don't know. He didn't say much, just sat there staring at the clouds and the water. Like he was listening to something nobody else could hear."

Sol laughed. "Sounds like someone I know. Probably make a good fisherman."

"The boy's only thirteen, Sol. He can't take over my license until he's sixteen. Three years is a long time. He'll discover girls pretty soon, if he hasn't already, and besides I was hoping to retire this year. The arthritis was really hurting this season. I don't think I can stay on the lake for another three years, waiting for him to decide."

"You going to sell it to Barings, then?"

"Maybe," Albert said with a shrug. "Lee Keung's expressed an interest so maybe I'll work the two of them against each other and take the best price."

"I'd rather Keung get it and have his brother out on the lake than one of Barings' boys. At least it'll still be an independent out there."

"Me too, but I don't want Keung to know that. If he wants it, he's going to have to work for it."

"Oh, Keung will have no problem with that. He'll work his ass off for another boat for his family. Wouldn't be the same though, without an Apetagon out on the lake."

Albert nodded, saying nothing but thinking about how he could find out if his grandson David was interested in going out on the lake.

Later, Sol steered the truck along the gravel road towards town and the main highway, several kilometres away. "Did you have a good day anyway?" he asked.

Albert grunted. "Not bad. Too many whitefish though. Filled four and half cartons, all of it whitefish."

"Not a sucker in the bunch, eh? Too bad too, Barings is paying good money for suckers."

"Always the same. Never fails. Whatever fish Barings pays the big bucks for always swims out to the centre of the lake and disappears while the no-money fish clog up our nets. Remember last year?" Albert asked. "Barings wasn't even buying suckers and there were suckers everywhere. I could have filled up my entire quota in two weeks if he was paying for them, but I caught a load of nothing."

"And not a single whitefish in sight."

"Except for now, when whitefish is 30 cents a pound."

"And suckers at four bucks. A pound."

"Yeah, but has anybody caught even two pounds in one day yet?"

"Not me, I know that."

"Me either. Why's he buying suckers for anyway this year. He never paid for suckers before."

"The Japanese my friend. The Japanese want 'em."

"What for?"

"To eat," Sol said with a laugh. "Canadian suckers direct from Lake Winnipeg are a delicacy over there, or so Barings says. So it's four bucks a pound for us."

"And about ten bucks a pound for him."

"That's the way it works," Sol said. "Barings' company got all the contacts with all the buyers and sellers round the world. All we do is catch the fish."

"Yeah, we do the hard part, while Barings, company gets all the money."

"I wouldn't know about that, Albert. Convincing the Japanese to pay $10 a pound for bottom feeders gotta be tough work."

"Yeah probably, but getting them to eat it was probably harder," Albert said with a laugh. "I think I'd rather be fishing." And he thought, maybe David would think the same thing one day.

2

The gravel road into town ran dead straight from the lake until a long slow curve, about a kilometre in length, turned the road 90 degrees to the south, so that it ran parallel to the lake. Just at the far lip of the curve, an unmarked T-intersection appeared in the trees, another gravel road leading into the first set of houses. Random gaps in the trees, the rusty husks of vehicles, discarded and dented garbage cans, droppings of glass from broken bottles and the odd malnourished stray dog divulged the location of lots, but little else could be seen from the road on this side of the town.

Just over 25 years ago, before Hydro built the little housing subdivision for its workers north of the river, there was nothing but trees and the homes for the trappers who ran lines along the northeast shore. Albert's former boss on the Keweetan, Jerry Harrison, used to have a cabin in these woods, in one of the small clearings. A narrow path used to wind from the mouth of the river where the Keweetan docked Sunday night, through the trees to his cabin.

Because Harrison was his boss, Albert never visited the man's cabin during the time they knew each other, except the one time.

It was an early Monday morning, just before the boat shipped out for Norman's Landing, and Harrison hadn't been seen for a week. The boat had even sailed without him the week before.

"He's probably sleeping off a drunk and I don't have time to wait for him," the Captain said. "Once you finish loading the barges, we'll push off. If he shows up by then, okay, but we aren't going to wait. I've got a schedule to keep."

Albert, Barings and Fency finished loading up the two barges that the Keweetan towed during its run around the lake, but Harrison still hadn't arrived. The boat pulled out without him and started on its way to Norman's Landing, the most northerly docking just south of Norway House. Albert, Barings and Fency stood on the lower deck of the stern and watched Grand Rapids fade into the distance.

"What do you think happened to him?" Albert asked.

"Just what the Captain said, he's sleeping off a drunk," Fency said with a laugh. "He's lucky if he doesn't get fired, and if he does, then that leaves you my friend", Fency slapped Barings on the shoulder, "as the next in line for crew chief."

"They won't fire Harrison," Barings said. "He's been on the Keweetan since the end of the war and crew chief for almost fifteen years."

"That means shit when you miss a sailing. Anybody who's missed a sailing since I've been here, has been fired," Fency said. "Harrison's gone for sure. And good riddance, too."

As much as he didn't like seeing someone getting fired, Albert quietly agreed that Harrison would not be missed. Jerry Harrison was a short, stocky man with pale, angry blue eyes and shocking white hair. Fency said Harrison's hair was so white because he was one of the first soldiers to hit Juno Beach on D-Day and his fear had turned his hair white. Fency never said where he had heard that story or who had told it to him, but insisted it was the truth. Albert wasn't sure he should believe the story 'cause Harrison never said anything about serving in the war, let alone landing on the beaches in Normandy. He never spoke to the crew on a personal basis: he simply barked and bellowed orders at them. "Come on you sons of bitches, how long does it take to load a fucking barge! Move your fucking asses before I kick them all the way across this lake!"

Harrison was a mean son of a bitch, and on Albert's first day working on the Keweetan, that's exactly what Harrison told him. "Make no mistake, Apetagon, I'm a mean son of a bitch. You fuck up and I'll fire your ass instantly, and even if we're on the middle of the lake I'll kick you off this fucking boat and you'll have to swim all the way back to your mother's tit in Norway House."

With Harrison gone, the seven days it took the Keweetan to tour the lake and return to Grand Rapids had been very quiet. There was no one screaming at the crew as they worked loading and unloading the barges when they docked or as they cleaned the boat from bow to stern when they were on the water. The amount of work they did was the same, but it didn't seem as hard when there wasn't someone constantly yelling. By the time the boat returned to Grand Rapids the following Sunday for their overnight stop, Albert was secretly wishing Jerry Harrison would get fired.

So when Harrison didn't show up that Monday morning, the Captain had a worried look on his face. Barings and Fency were below deck, bringing a load of coal to the engine room, leaving Albert alone at the dock with the Captain. "Did you boys happen to run into him in town last night?" the captain asked Albert.

Albert shook his head. "I was only in town for a couple of hours last night, but I didn't see him, Sir," he said. "And Barings and Fency didn't say anything to me about running into him."

"That's strange," the captain whispered. He rubbed his beard with his right hand, his eyes searching the forest for any sort of sign. "Do you know where he lives, Albert?"

Albert pointed to a small path that lead into the trees. "I know he runs a winter trapline north of the river, so I'm guessing his cabin's over that way. I've never been there myself, but I've seen him heading that way."

The Captain nodded, and after several seconds he gave Albert a quiet command. "I'd like you to head over to his house."

"Me, Sir?" Albert asked pointing at his own chest.

"Yes, Albert. I'd like it if you'd go to Mr. Harrison's house and find him."

"What if I can't find his house?"

"Just follow the path you said you've seen him walk down. Shouldn't be that many houses out there."

Albert looked to the path and then back to the Captain. "What should I say to him if I find him?"

The Captain cleared his throat and then spat into the lake. "Tell him if he doesn't show up for work today, he's fired." Albert felt his stomach tighten but the Captain gave him a little smile. "Make sure you tell him that those words come from me and not you. Tell him that you're just delivering my message and if he gives you any lip, then tell him to come talk to me. You got that Albert?"

Despite what the Captain had said, Albert's stomach didn't relax. Still, he nodded in response to the

Captain's command. "Yes Sir. I'll go try to find Mr. Harrison."

"Good then. I'll get the rest of the boys to finish the loading while you're gone. We push off in an hour so hurry it up." Albert nodded again and slowly headed towards the trees.

The path was a dark, dank place with just tiny snatches of sunlight forcing their way through the canopy of leaves above. Albert tried to keep an even pace through the woods but he couldn't. The floor of the forest wasn't level — thick roots bulged through the grass like lumps in a carpet. There were grassy soft spots where water seeped deep into the earth and a few bits of snow lingering where the sun would never find them, making his steps erratic and irregular. Several times he lost his balance and had to grab at trees, the urine-coloured sap still fresh and sticky. A gauntlet of branches and leaves clawed at him and a layer of crisp dampness settled into his clothes. His body began to shiver and his teeth started to chatter. Battalions of mosquitoes swirled around him, darting at his exposed hands and neck. Mosquitoes normally didn't bother him. Grand Rapids' bugs were no match for the voracious creatures in his hometown of Norway House, but this time he slapped at every tiny sting and waved at the high-pitched whines. He stumbled through the trail like a hunted animal, his heart pounding and his lungs gasping. He pushed and shoved his way through until he tripped and fell, striking his knee on a rock and sending a bright flash of pain up his leg.

When his head cleared and the pain subsided to a tolerable level, Albert found himself in a small clearing of soft tall grasses. The sun, no longer obscured by trees, shone bright and warm. The coolness lifted out of Albert and most of the mosquitoes retreated back into the cool, dark forest. Albert looked about and in the centre of the clearing, sitting on a small rise in the land, was Jerry Harrison's tiny box of a house. Each wall was about twelve feet long and built with various wood beams, two by fours and pieces of old boxes with the labeling still visible. The roof was a series of grated iron sheets lashed together with thick tangles of twine and nailed to the tops of the walls with long thin and rusted nails. The entire building leaned to the east.

Albert pushed himself up, and limped to the house. A breeze whistled through the trees and made the old wood in the shack groan in protest. A background hum — the buzzing of flies — hung in the air. "Jerry?" Albert asked. A feeling of discomfort rose in him; he'd had always called Jerry Sir, Mister or the longer Mister Harrison.

There was no answer, so he rapped lightly on the wall, afraid that he might knock the building down. "Hey Jerry. You home?" Albert said a little louder. Again he waited for an answer, but there was none. A gust of wind blew and the entire shack creaked as it leaned with the breeze. The buzz of flies became louder as Albert circled to what he figured was the front of the house. "Hey Jerry. The boat's sailing in less than an hour and the Captain says if you don't make this week's sailing he's going to fire you. Jerry? You hear me?"

Albert walked up to the door and gave it a couple of gentle knocks. "Jerry? You in there?" He knocked three more times, each one slightly harder. "Come on Jerry, if you're in there, you better answer. The Captain's really pissed about you missing last week's sailing, but he's ready to forget about it if you make today's and give a good reason why you didn't make it last week. I know you can't be running your traps 'cause it's way too early in the season so you gotta be home . . . " Albert let his voice drift away, and after a deep breath he grabbed the door handle and tried to lift it. A piece of rusted metal snapped off the handle and Abert's hand slipped upwards, the fleshy part of his thumb scraping against the wood and snagging a few slivers. Albert jerked back from the door as the barbed bristles pierced his thumb and he did a little dance of pain, hopping from foot to foot, snapping the wrist of his injured hand back and forth trying to shake away the splinters and pain. "Goddamn it Jerry!" he shouted. "What's your fucking problem?"

Albert stormed back to the door and shoved against it with his shoulder. It scraped against the floor, but even with all his weight behind it, he only managed to get it a third of the way open. Albert pressed harder, but wasn't able to force the door any further. He leaned around the door and looked into the room. It was dark, with sunlight slicing through the wall and striking the floor. The smell of tired, old air and rotting meat drifted into his nose. The buzz of flies grew louder and he heard something small scurry out of the room, digging and scratching against a far corner of the house . . . and then it was gone, its scrabbling footsteps darting across the grass towards the forest. Albert shivered slightly, but unlike the forest, there was no layer of coolness in the cabin. He stepped through the door and stood at the entrance. Thick pelts hung off every wall like elaborate curtains. In the centre of the room was a black wood stove, the black pipe climbing to the roof. An old wooden rocking chair and a short wooden table, about one foot square, were situated near the stove, directly near the front to offer easy access to heat, to ease the addition of wood to the fire and help in the preparation of food. A black pot and percolator stood next to each other on the top of the stove. There were more pelts stacked three feet high behind the door and beside this was a shorter stack of about three or four pelts. An old sack, probably a pillow, Albert reasoned, and a blanket with the distinctive Hudson Bay strips, were rolled up at the end of this stack. Articles of clothing were strewn on and around the bed.

Albert approached the stove and looked inside the pot. There was a thick layer of black sludge, and through the overpowering smell of rotten meat he could pick up the slight smell of burnt potatoes and meat — some type of stew, he guessed. Albert gingerly touched the pot, but the metal was cool. The same with the percolator. He lifted the lid of the coffeemaker and saw even more sludge; the bitter smell of powerful coffee hit his nose.

It was then that he noticed the clump that looked like a pile of old clothes against the far wall. Without taking his eyes off of it, he set down the percolator and walked around the stove. He approached the clump and softly kicked it. A cloud of angry flies burst into the air and buzzed around him. There was some give from the kick, but not the kind he expected from an old clump of clothing. Something fleshy. Albert's heart started to pound and he caught his breath when he realized what the clump was. He forced himself to one knee and placed his hand on it. The coldness of the body sent a quick shiver through him but he quickly pulled on the cloth. Jerry Harrison's body rolled onto its back, the arms flopping like rags. The neck moved a half second behind the body and, as if in slow motion, the head twisted around to face Albert. Jerry Harrison's face was as grey as an overcast day. The eyeless sockets and gaping mouth stared up at him. Ants, beetles and other bugs scurried across the dead skin.

Albert jumped back — "Jesus fucking Christ!" — bumped into the stove and knocked over the pot and percolator. The coffee and food splattered against the floor, spraying against the wall and the bed of pelts. Albert covered his mouth with his hand, and step by step — eyes frozen to Jerry's face, a free arm reaching behind him — staggered backwards across the room. He finally felt the wood of the door and with all his strength dragged it open, the wood screeching and splintering in protest. Sunlight came into the room, almost tentatively, like a cautious animal. But even in the light of day Albert saw only decay and emptiness. The atmosphere was suffocating, like living underwater. There seemed to be no light, even when there was light. There seemed to be no air, even though there was air. He couldn't believe that someone actually lived in this place, and not just any person, someone he knew. Jerry Harrison wasn't a family member, he wasn't even somebody Albert would call a friend. But still . . . for the past couple of years, he was somebody Albert saw every day. As Albert saw it, they were at least close.

Albert gave the dead man another look and he could almost hear Harrison's voice calling out from behind his eye sockets. "What the fuck are your staring at Apetagon?"

Albert shook his head to clear the vision and jumped out of the room. The gush of fresh air and sunlight gave him such a sense of escape and freedom that he collapsed to his knees and emptied his stomach on the grass. When there was nothing left he dry heaved. Finally, after catching his breath and gathering his strength, Albert climbed to his feet and headed back to the boat so he could tell the Captain that Jerry wasn't coming to work anymore.

3

The trail to Jerry Harrison's cabin was long gone but Albert figured his trailer was almost in the exact spot where Harrison's cabin had been. It was situated in a lot hidden behind a line of trees the Hydro company either forgot to or didn't feel like cutting down. Albert's truck also sat in that lot, a fuel pump problem that if he didn't get to himself, or talk Fency's boy into fixing for him, it'd become just another one of those rusted husks. Fency's boy wouldn't have a problem coming out and fixing the fuel pump on Albert's truck; he'd probably do it for a six-pack. "Or if you got no beers, Albert, I'll do it for old time's sake," Fency said the last time he did some work on Albert's vehicle.

Albert grunted a laugh. "Old times sake? You're not old enough for old time's sake."

"Then how 'bout old time's sake for you and my old man?"

Albert nodded and smiled. "Fair enough."

The road from the lake went another hundred yards and hit another intersection, but there was still little appearance of a town. There was another 90-degree curve, this time quick sharp — Albert held onto the door frame to prevent sliding into Sol — and the forest abruptly ended, exposing the centre of town. Downtown Grand Rapids, as some jokingly called it, was a simple clearing with a newly-paved two-lane highway slicing it in half, and several roads branching off in various directions. For the first 25 metres off the highway, every road was paved, and then they became gravel further down. Several buildings ran along the length of the highway. Half of them were empty, surrounded by tall grass and every single pane of glass broken out. Some of the broken windows were covered with plywood, but most were left bare, a few of them sanctuaries for birds, mice and other small mammals.

If you drove north from Winnipeg the first major attractions you'd hit in the centre of Grand Rapids were the two bridges, although only one still spanned the river. The older bridge, built for the old highway, was once a three-truss bridge. Now, just one truss sat in the middle of the river, disconnected and alone, an island of pale green, rust-spotted girders that were now homes for pelicans, seagulls and other birds, a diving platform for kids in the summer, and a smoking and drinking hangout in the winter. Back in the days when it had traversed the river, the old bridge had no space underneath for larger boats and float planes — there had

been a larger dock to the right of the mouth of the river
— and barely any room for smaller boats like Albert's.
You could get under it, but you had to duck your head,
cut your engine and allow your momentum to carry you
under.

The new bridge, built of solid white concrete a few
years ago when they repaved the highway, arched high
and long over the river, the lowest point about two
meters higher than the highest point of the old bridge.
The new bridge held two lanes for traffic and one
sidewalk for pedestrians and bikes. It also allowed for
almost any sort of river and lake craft to pass under, and
the main dock for boats and planes had been moved
further upriver.

The second landmark that announced the town of
Grand Rapids was the newly constructed Grand Rapids
Motel, built around the same time the new bridge was
erected. It sat just on the north side of the bridge, a
quick right off the main highway. The motel was a
sixteenroom building with an office, compact and
square, its colour of pale industrial yellow revealing that
it was constructed directly from the box.

On the opposite side of the highway were the Grand
Rapids bar, an L-shaped box of weather-beaten wood,
and the Esso gas station, convenience store and restaurant, painted in its trademarked blue and white,
kitty-corner from the motel.

The main sight to see in town, and the reason why
Grand Rapids was built in the first place, was the mouth
of the Saskatchewan River. It emptied out into a small
bay that marked the beginning of Lake Winnipeg.

The river began its life as two rivers, two provinces over. The North started in the Rocky Mountains, at the bottom end of some glacier near Mount Forbes, while the South started in the empty flat prairie of Southern Alberta, when the Oldman hit the Bow. They both weaved through Alberta, into southern Saskatchewan, the South heading north to met up with its partner just east of Prince Albert. Together, they continued through to Manitoba until they hit the big lake. Before the dam was built just upriver of Grand Rapids, the final miles of the Saskatchewan were wild. The river boiled and swirled into the biggest and most dangerous rapids west of Hudson Bay until one final plunge of white foam, mist and whirlpools. So much oxygen was created in those last rapids that fish, insects, plants and all manner of life were attracted to the scene. And then, after the final blast, the river settled, content with age, a flowing lake almost two kilometres wide, it ran right into Lake Winnipeg.

Man, first the natives and then the Europeans, were attracted to the river's mouth. The flat land and the fresh water, abundant trees and unlimited fish, made it an ideal stopping point for a voyage west. The grand rapids, as they came to be called, also forced earlier settlers to rest up before they attempted the great portage needed to circumnavigate the rapids to calmer waters. With time, more of these travelers, no longer happy with the arduous journeys to the west, started to fish, hunt, cut wood, trap and trade in fur, food or any other services they had to offer. Soon, they named the town after its greatest asset, the grand rapids. As the years passed, the town grew, reached a peak and then settled into a comfortable life. Voyager canoes were replaced by York boats and then by larger craft, steam, then diesel. The town still traded with what they were provided with and lived quietly into and through most of the twentieth century.

Attracted by the power of the river, engineers from Hydro, along with local and distant politicians, visited the rapids and agreed on the project. The biggest dam in the country at the time. It took ten years to build, employed thousands of people, and created a larger town with more amenities. It also created a road, direct to Winnipeg and points south, for supplies and more people to work on the dam. When the dam was completed, the rapids that were responsible for the name and creation of the town were replaced by a reservoir, along with a number of upriver settlements. The power of the river became the power of electricity, enough to power all the towns and cities in Manitoba, with enough left over to sell to the Americans in North and South Dakota, Minnesota, Wisconsin and anybody who asked. Below the dam, the river flowed a little slower and less deep, but was still almost two kilometres wide. And if they weren't careful in controlling the flow through the dam, the river could still flood parts of Grand Rapids.

Several houses also sat in the centre of town, but only two — one on the same property as the Esso station — were occupied. The first, directly behind the station housed Lee Keung, owner of the Esso, his wife, his three kids, two mothers-in-law, a couple of uncles and a brother and sister. Keung's family grew by one every two years or so as they were able to save enough money to bring another member over from Korea. Keung's brother, who worked for Manitoba Hydro, started to bring his wife and his kids and other members of his family. Soon they would need their own home and they were eyeing the other bungalow which sat on the same property but further back, almost into the trees. This home, an identical version of the Keung's house but in worse condition, was home to Fency's boy, who like Albert and Sol made his money fishing during the season and did odd jobs during the rest of the year. Fency's boy had a standing contract with the Keung's as their resident mechanic, a service they offered to people whose cars would break down on the highway which were then towed into Grand Rapids. Although the family did not entirely approve of Fency's relationship with their eldest daughter Irma, her leaving for university in this September seemed very timely. Fency would no doubt follow her there, leaving the bungalow and selling his boat and license to Keung's brother, giving the family a place to live and possibly another source of income to bring more family members over. All the other houses near the highway were long empty, many since the late 60s when Manitoba Hydro built new housing for its dam workers on the north side of the highway, away from the river and its flood plain, and the rest since the early 80s when the Band built new houses for treaty members on the south side of the highway, along the river, directly on the flood plain.

4

Sol pulled the truck into the parking lot of the Grand Rapids bar, the gravel crunching underneath his tires. A portable marquee, still attached to its trailer, stood at the edge of the highway entrance to the parking lot announcing: G AND APIDS LOUNGE & TAVE N POKE /BLCKJCK VLTS OFFSLAES LIQUO & BEER OPEN TIL TWO. The letter on the end of the word beer used to be a B, but became an R with a diagonal line drawn in black marker. Along the front side of the bar, unstained plywood sheets covered what used to be four ground-level windows. Neon beer-signs hung in the spaces in front of the plywood and then metal gratings hung in front of the signs to prevent vandalism or theft or both. The front door of the bar was made of thick translucent plexiglass with half-inch, horizontal grating behind the glass. The words NO MINORS, were stencilled on a sheet of solid white plastic and hung above the door. The bar opened at 11 a.m. and closed at 2:30 a.m. with last call a half hour earlier. It served hard liquor, bottled beer, one type of draught and a few simple shooters. The bar sold smokes, some junk food, simple bar food like burgers, fries, microwaved chicken fingers and movie nachos and cheese, and gave away free popcorn from a self-service machine.

Sol parked his truck next to others similar in style and model, and all covered in a pale layer of dust. He and Albert climbed out of the vehicle and walked into the front door.

When they walked through the front door, Albert and Sol still had not yet entered the bar. There was a separate entrance area installed so that people just wanting to buy offsale or smokes didn't have to actually enter the bar to do so.

The initial entry area was a box of a room about 25 square feet in area. Directly across the front door was a counter about chest high and a large sheet of clear plexiglass all the way to the ceiling, reinforced by a criss-crossing pattern of metal framing. There were only two breaks in the glass: a circular hole, cut in at eye level, about four inches in diameter; and a rectangular one, cut flush with the counter, about half a metre long and three inches high. The front entrance area was brightly lit by three fluorescent tubes.

Norma McLeod, a short, chunky woman with dark native features and straight, jet black hair pulled into two braids, sat on a stool behind the glass. Her feet swung in the air and her thick horn-rimmed glasses hung at the edge of her nose as she read a thick Archie comic book. Norma's room was about twice as large as the front hallway and all along the walls were various liquor bottles: rum, vodka, rye, whiskey, tequila — the basics — and a few luxuries, Baileys, Khalua, Grand Marnier and a few additional bottles of mostly domestic white wine. There was also the odd bottle of red wine and maybe a couple bottles of champagne. The two side walls were covered with six-packs, 12s and 24s of beer of various types, mostly brewed by major Canadian breweries — Canadian, Blue, Bud, Draft, Coors and Coors light — and a few imported American beers, Old Milwaukee, Miller and the like. At the front of the counter was a computerized cash register and on the front of that was a sign: Pay Here! Pick up Beer in Bar!

On the counter behind the glass sat the remains of a hamburger, a small pile of fries and a glob of ketchup next to a half-full glass of cola and ice. Every few seconds Norma would casually reach for a fry, dip it into the ketchup and slide it into her mouth.

"Hey Norma," Sol said, leaning his elbows on the counter. Albert stood behind, looking at the bright bottles of liquor.

Norma looked up and her black eyes brightened. She quickly wiped her face and smiled without opening her mouth. She twisted towards the glass. "Hey Sol," she asked. "Where you been? Haven't seen you in at least a week? I was starting to miss you."

Sol laughed. "You're the only one Norma. Even Albert here didn't say he missed me."

Norma nodded, registering Albert's presence. "Hey Albert. Good fishing today?"

Albert returned Norma's greeting with his own nod. "Not really, only four cartons. Pretty slim," he said. "How 'bout you, Norma? How you doin'?"

"Keeping busy, you know. How's Elaine? Haven't seen her today yet."

"I don't know. You know Elaine, probably working her ass off at the restaurant."

"Yeah, place probably couldn't run without her."

"That's what she likes to believe."

"That Keung would go out of business if it wasn't for her."

"I doubt it. He'd just get one of his kids to take her place. Make more money 'cause he wouldn't have to pay 'em."

"Or he'd just get another one of his relatives from Korea to come in and run the place," Sol added. "Who's in attendance today, Norma?"

"Pretty much everybody today," Norma said, and then paused. "Even Abe."

Sol straightened. "Abe? What's he doing here?"

Norma was about to speak, but Albert beat her to it. "Last day of the season, Sol. Abe always has a few drinks last day of the season. Everybody does."

Norma nodded. "Every fisherman in town probably in there today. Even the company boys."

Albert slapped Sol on the shoulder. "You're out of town all the time talking with Hydro you forget what the hell's going on in town."

"Heck. I've been working for the folks in the town, you know," Sol said defensively. "All those fishermen in town are going to thank me for all the work I've done. You too Norma, you're going to be mighty grateful that I was spending all those days out of town dealing with Hydro."

Norma leaned forward, her face lighting up like a little kid discovering a new toy. "So it's true then. Hydro signed the IBA?"

Sol nodded. "Damn right they did. Took a long time of talking, but those bastards finally decided that if they wanted to upgrade the dam, they'd better be nice to us or we were going to fuck up their regulatory process."

"Did you guys get the retro money for when they flooded the land without asking us?"

"You know I can't tell you that, Norma," Sol said. "Just come to the meeting tonight and you'll find out."

"But I can't come to any meeting tonight. It's bingo night. Why the hell did you schedule a meeting on bingo night anyways?"

Sol shrugged. "I told the Joe B. not to schedule the meeting tonight. That's just what I said. 'It's Bingo night Joe, most the women and a good chunk of the men aren't going to come to the meeting because it's bingo night.' And do you know what old Joe B. said to me? You know what he said to me?" Sol turned to Albert and pointed. "He was one of your old friends wasn't he Albert? Didn't you go to school with Joe B. back in Norway House?"

"That was his cousin Joey," Albert said shaking his head. "Different guy, same name."

"All right then." Sol turned to back to Norma, leaning an elbow on the counter. "But you know what Joe B. said to me when I told him that he was scheduling the meeting the same night as bingo night? Go ahead, ask me if you want to know what he said?"

"You were there Sol, I wasn't," Albert said. "I have no idea what he said."

"Well. Joe B. says to me, and I know you'll find this funny Norma, but he says, no word of a lie: 'Some things are more important than bingo, Sol.'"

Norma clasped her hands to her mouth to stifle a laugh. Albert smiled and chuckled. "He actually said that?" Norma demanded. "He actually said that some things are more important than bingo! Joe B. The Chief! Actually said that? Out loud? In public?"

"No word of a lie," Sol said, placing his left hand on his heart and raising his right. "Joe B. actually told me that some things are more important than bingo."

"Now I've heard everything," Norma said with a huff. "Some things are more important than bingo. Who does that man think he is?"

"Like you said Norma, he's the chief," Sol said.

Norma tapped her finger angrily against the plexi-glass. "Not for long. Not if he keeps saying stupid things like that he won't be. I'll make sure of that."

"That's what I told him. I said, 'Joe B., promise me you'll never say that to anyone else or you'll never be chief again.'"

"Well good for you Sol. If it wasn't for you, Joe B wouldn't know anything going on in this town." Norma slapped a hand on top of the counter, her voice getting angrier. Sol backed away from the glass to give her room. "Where the hell is Joe B.'s head for saying some things are more important the bingo? What kind of chief says things like that?" Norma sputtered for a couple of seconds, almost choking. She grabbed her glass of coke and took a couple of sips to clear the clog in her throat. Albert and Sol said nothing while they waited for her to calm down. When she regained composure, she continued. "And you know what else bugs me about him: what the hell kind of name is Joe B.? Huh? What the hell is that? Who the hell calls their kid Joe B.? Is that a real name or did he make it up? Sol do you know? Is that his real name or not?"

Sol shrugged and turned to Albert. He spoke in a calm voice. "You know the family better than most, Albert. Is Joe B. Joe B.'s real name?"

"His real name is Joe but like I told you, I went to school with his cousin Joey," Albert began. "But Joey and Joe B. are only a couple of months apart and the rest of the family had trouble telling them apart. I don't know why, Joey was always a scrawny kid and Joe B., well you guys know what he looks like. Scrawny isn't a word you'd use to describe Joe B. But so they could make sure which one was which, they started calling the oldest one Joe. A. and the younger one Joe B. But after awhile, everybody figured that Joe A. sounded like Joey anyway so they just started calling him that."

"Then why didn't they just start calling Joe B. Joe?" Norma asked. "That would make more sense. Why do they still call him Joe B.?"

Albert shrugged. "I don't know. They've always been kind of a weird family."

Norma nodded in agreement. "No wonder he's such a messed-up chief scheduling the IBA meeting on bingo night," Norma said with a tsk. "Couldn't you talk him out of it Sol? You know nobody's going to be there."

"He insisted that we had to schedule the meeting tonight because we just signed the IBA the other day," Sol said. "He said we shouldn't wait to tell the people the good news."

"Well there's going to be nobody there to hear the good news," Norma said. "So you might as well tell me, anyway. That way I can pass on the info to everybody at the bingo tonight. Did you get the retro IBA that you were going for?"

Sol looked about as if he was being watched. Then he leaned forward and whispered, "I can't give you the details . . . but . . . Yeah, we got the retro IBA."

Norma clapped her hands in delight and started spinning on her stool, sending her leftover fries and burger flying to the floor. Her anger at Joe B. for scheduling the meeting on bingo night was replaced with pure glee. "Woweee! I'm going to get me a new car! I'm going to get me a new car! Yeehaa!" Norma started singing. "I'm going to get a new car, I'm going to get a new car . . . "

Albert and Sol looked at each and then shrugged. "Let's go in and say hi to the boys," Sol said, and turned to enter the bar. "See ya Norma."

"Take it easy, Norma," Albert said, but she paid little attention to them. She was still spinning and singing her new-car song as Albert followed Sol into the bar.

5

Compared to the front hallway, the bar was dark, no fluorescents, just incandescent bulbs hanging from the ceiling and surrounded by fake stained-glass shades. The bar was basically a large square with an additional section added onto the opposite wall to make a stubby L. The addition was just a makeshift stage with black speakers on each side and lights on the ceiling. The bar itself, made from fake mahogany with the coolers of beer behind and glasses hanging above, stretched along the wall just to the left of the entrance. A copper bar about four inches in diameter ran three inches from the bottom of the bar, serving as a footrest. The room was full of round tables, many of them pushed into groups. Every chair looked taken, most of them by company fishermen, sitters and standers grouped in a circle near the bar. Sol's brother Abe, Fency's boy and a couple of other independents sat around tables near the centre of the room, sipping from bottles of beer. The din of conversation floated in the air, along with the green smell of the lake and the stale scent of fish. Most of the conversation came from the large group of company fishermen. They laughed uproariously at some joke and then splintered into smaller groups of conversation. Albert and Sol waited at the door for their eyes to adjust.

"I think she likes you," Albert said.

"Who?"

"Norma. I really think she likes you."

Sol turned. "Yeah, Norma and me used to date in high school, that was long before you moved down from Norway House, but she married Charlie Mason instead."

"Charlie died three years ago, Sol. Cancer got him."

"I know. I was at the funeral."

"Then later you should go say hi to Norma. Talk about old times."

Sol smiled at Albert and then waved him off. "Go play your games, Albert. Stay outta mine."

As Sol moved towards his brother's table, Lesley Ghostkeeper, one of the company men, shouted at him. "Hey Sol! Come on over!"

Sol waved. "Sorry Les, gonna say hi to my brother."

"Oh come on Sol. Come on over. The company's buying."

Sol continued towards the independents. "You know I can't be seen with the likes of you until I've got at least several beers in my belly."

"Your loss," Ghostkeeper said. He turned to his group and whispered something. They looked up at Sol and then broke into laughter. Sol smiled. "But I'll take your beer," he shouted, waving to Jake, the tall lanky Indian who acted as the daytime bartender. "Couple rounds of beers for the real fishermen, Jake," Sol said, and pointed to the table of independents. "And put it on the company's tab. You heard Les, they're buying." Jake nodded once and bent down to the coolers to retrieve the order. The company fishermen went quiet and Albert smiled, knowing that they could not refuse to pay for all those beers since they had offered them in the first place. Sol also pointed towards Albert, smiling. They made eye contact and Sol raised his eyebrows slightly. "And don't forget Albert." Jake waved from below the bar, acknowledging the addition to the order. Sol raised his eyebrows again and turned to his brother's table, ignoring the stunned stares from some of the company fishermen and the slight smiles of satisfaction from the others. Sol sat down at the table, getting a slap on the back from Fency's boy. The younger fisherman whispered something in Sol's ear and the two of them laughed. The other Jacks brother, Abe, an older, greyer, but almost identical version of Sol, glared across the table at his younger brother. Conversation in the bar began again, and then slowly built to its previous level. Albert watched for a second and turned to the games.

There were seven machines lined up along the right wall of the bar. Each one offered you three games: poker, blackjack and slots. Somewhere Albert had read that in Las Vegas your best odds for winning came from playing poker. All other games, especially the slots or roulette, were simply designed to take your money away from you. Blackjack gave you some control over the game, but you played against the dealer and though he had to stay on 17 or hit on 16, you lost some of that control. With poker, the cards were random, but you played against no one and your winnings were based on the kind of hand you ended up with. A high pair returned your bet, usually a credit; two pairs, double your bet; three of a kind, triple; a flush or straight, five times; full-house, ten times; and four of a kind, 25 times.

Albert walked up to the first machine, reached into his pocket for his twoonie and sat down on the stool. Sitting at the game next to him was Jerry Johnson, a tiny man with fading grey hair and a long bony face. He wore a white dress shirt buttoned to the top, his sleeveless undershirt visible through the fabric. A black tie hung from his neck and cufflinks kept his sleeves buttoned. His trousers were pressed to a straight sharp seam, and the colour of the pants matched the colour of his tie. His shoes looked recently shined even though they had a few spots of mud and dirt. Jerry Johnson seemed dressed for church and in a sense it was true. The VLTs were his altar and every day from one to four p.m. he made his offerings.

Jerry suffered from severe arthritis and his hands curled out and back from his wrists, making a slight S. His fingers bent tightly at the knuckles and pulled inward to his palms. He always kept a loose pile of coins on the right counter that separated his machine from the next, and since none of his fingers functioned well enough, he had to reach both hands into the stack of coins and pick up one coin at a time by pressing his hands together at the base of his pinkies. His entire body stiffened as he slowly pulled the coin towards the machine. He pushed from his feet and rose slightly from the stool, his chest directly over the buttons and his head almost touching the screen. Beads of sweat formed on his forehead and he emitted a low hum from the back of his throat. Finally, his hands pulled apart and the coin fell, a tiny electronic chime announcing its arrival. He'd repeat the ritual until he was satisfied with the number of the credits on the machine.

When he was ready Jerry said, "Hey Albert." The voice came from deep in his throat, a dry rasp.

"Hey Jerry," Albert said. "How they playing?"

Jerry shrugged. "Not bad. Nothing too spectacular but nothing too terrible. Mostly evening out. How many you playing today?" Jerry asked.

"Not sure yet. I was thinking maybe twenty bucks or so."

"Big day."

"Last day of the season. Thought I'd celebrate a bit. Maybe bring in some extra money before heading home."

"Oh, that's why everybody's still around. Knew it had to be special. Specially with Abe in the bar."

"You can always tell something's special when Abe's in the bar."

Jerry nodded. "So, you have a good day on the lake or what?"

Albert shrugged, "Nothing too spectacular, but nothing too terrible," and dropped his first twoonie into the machine. The chime sounded, telling him he had two credits. He tapped the start button with one hand while grabbing his beer with the other. He took a sip and his cards were dealt in front of him: two eights, a ten, a seven and a six. Albert got rid of all the cards except the two eights. The machines didn't mind giving out a few pairs and a three of a kind, but rarely spotted

Wayne Arthurson

you a straight or a flush. The machine offered him only three crap cards. "Shit," he muttered. He hit deal again and once more he was given a low pair with the chance of a straight. He was ready to drop the crap and save the pair when Jerry spoke. "Forget the pair, go for the straight."

Albert's hand hung above a button and he looked over. Jerry was intently playing his own game.

"Go for the straight?" Albert asked. "Really?"

"Really," Jerry said.

"Why? The machines never give straights."

"Yours will . . . today."

"Why just mine?"

"I was all ready to play that game today, but I accidentally sat down here. Too late to get up," Jerry said. "Pissed me off too because that machine's been due for weeks."

"You should know." Albert moved his hand to discard one card from his low pair and take his chances on the straight, but one of Jerry's gnarled hands came up slowly and rested itself, like a moth, on Albert's forearm. Albert looked over and Jerry was staring at him. Jerry's eyes were grey and through his thick bottle glasses Albert saw that they were the exact colour of the lake on those days when the deep heavy clouds were reflecting off it. It was like Jerry carried his 35 years of fishing on the lake inside his eyes. "Of course I'm not responsible for any of your losses if my advice doesn't pan out," Jerry said.

Albert shook his head. "Wouldn't think of it. It's my choice whether I listen to you or not."

Jerry blinked very slowly, the lake in his eyes disappearing for a second and then returning, thick and grey. "Just so you know. I'm not responsible."

Albert gingerly placed his hand on Jerry's. He could feel the sharp, brittle bones trembling through the skin. "I wouldn't hold you responsible for any decision I made Jerry, even if you did give me advice."

Jerry nodded and slowly pulled his hand away. He returned to his game. "Just so you know."

"I know," Albert said. He discarded one card from the low pair and waited the second it took the machine to drop the next card.

About fifteen minutes later, Albert pushed away from machine, holding the tiny chit sheet showing him and Jake the bartender how much he was owed in winnings. He swallowed the last bit of beer and set it down on the counter. "Told you the straights were paying off," Jerry said without looking up. "Better for you than me."

"Sometimes you get lucky," Albert said, reaching into his pocket. He pulled out a twoonie and dropped it into Jerry's pile of coins. Jerry glanced at the coin and then slowly looked to Albert. "What's that for?"

"Nothing, just a little bit of change for the advice."

Jerry looked back at the coin. "I said I wasn't responsible for the machines."

"You only said losses. Nobody said anything about winnings. Your advice paid off, so I thought I — "

Jerry cut him off. "The advice was free, Albert. I don't give it to everybody but when I do, I don't take responsibility, lose or win."

Albert placed his hand on Jerry's shoulder. The bones stiffened and trembled beneath his palm. "Have I ever borrowed money from you Jerry? You know, when we were both fishing, before your arthritis made you quit, or long ago when we were working for Hydro on the dam."

Jerry's shoulder relaxed slightly. "That was a long time ago," he whispered.

"Yeah, but I probably borrowed something from you. Maybe at lunch or after work or something, maybe like today, at the end of the season. I know I had to have borrowed some money a few times over the years. God knows, I've borrowed money from pretty much everybody in this town."

"Yeah, maybe," Jerry said with a sigh.

"Then chances are I still owe you."

"Yeah," Jerry said. "But what if I owe you? Maybe I borrowed from you."

"Maybe you did. No, you probably did."

"Well then maybe I owe you."

Albert shrugged. "Then if you do, or if I do or whatever, then with this twoonie here, we'll call it even."

"Even!" Jerry sputtered. "We can't just call everything even with a twoonie."

"Why not? We'd both be going to our graves knowing at least for sure you and I were square. After 30 years of working together on the lake and the dam, seeing most of our kids getting born, going to all those weddings and funerals, we'd be even-steven. Not many people would be able to say that after 30 years of knowing and working with someone that they were completely square with them."

Jerry shook his head. "Yeah, but I might owe you more than that and you'd be getting gypped. Or worse, you might owe me more than all that and I might be getting gypped. I don't want to feel like I'm getting gypped or make you feel like you're getting gypped."

Albert took a deep breath. "Shit Jerry, why can't you just take the fucking twoonie!" he snapped. "It's no big deal!"

"If it's no big deal then why all that shit about 30 years of weddings and funerals and calling it all even-steven with a twoonie?"

"I only said that so you'd take the fucking twoonie. I didn't think you'd make a federal case out of it."

"Why'd you give me the twoonie in the first place then?"

"I don't know. Maybe 'cause all those straights you suggested would pay off, did pay off, and I thought I'd thank you for it."

"Why not buy me a couple of beers then?"

"Would you accept a couple of beers?"

"What for?"

"For your advice on the machine."

"I told you Albert, I don't take responsibility for my advice on the VLTs."

"Why not?"

Jerry paused and then turned back to his machine. He hit the button and the game dealt him his five cards "'Cause in my experience, it usually causes a lot of trouble."

"No shit," Albert said. He turned away from the VLT's.

As he walked away, Jerry shouted at him: "What about the twoonie, Albert? What about the twoonie?"

Albert ignored Jerry and sat down at the table with Sol, Abe and Fency's boy. The other independents who had been sitting there had moved over to the company table and it was difficult to tell which fisherman was independent and which worked for Barings' company. Sol slid a glass of beer across the table. Albert took it and drank half.

"What's with Jerry?" Sol asked.

"Jerry's fucked in the head," Albert said.

"If you ask me, he spends too much time with those machines," Abe said quietly. "The worst thing they ever did to this bar was install those goddamned VLTs in here. Someone like Jerry Johnson should be hanging around with his grandkids."

"His grandkids are probably Fency's age," Sol said, pointing at the younger fisherman. "Am I right? His grandkids must be your age?"

Fency's face was just starting to show the fisherman wrinkles near the eyes, but the rest of his face was unblemished. He had a short, flat nose and his eyes, slightly slanted, seemed only half open. His hair was short underneath his Lund ballcap and soft, dark stubble grew down his face and under his nose and chin. A slab of scar tissue peeked under the left side of the stubble, ran down the side of his neck and then disappeared into his shirt. Fency shook his head. "'Bout ten years younger."

"Really? You figure an old guy like Jerry's got older grandkids," Sol said.

"Jerry's not that old," Albert said. "It's the arthritis."

"Well, he's got to be in his 70s at least."

Albert and Abe shook their heads. "Early 60s," Abe said. "Not too much older than me and Albert."

"No shit," Sol said. "But some of his grandkids got kids, don't they?"

"Yeah, a couple," Fency answered.

"One of them with one of my grandkids," Albert said. "Jackie and Earl. Seventeen years old the two of them and they got themselves a two year old."

Sol sat up in his chair, smiling. "I didn't know you and Jerry were related."

"We're not. Our grandkids just had a kid together."

"That doesn't make you related?" Sol asked. Fency and Abe shook their heads.

"No, it just means a couple of our grandkids had a kid," Albert said.

"Boy or girl?" Sol asked.

"I don't know, boy I think?"

"You don't know? How can you not know?" Sol asked with a look of surprise on his face.

"I got eighteen grandkids and I can't even remember the names of all of them so you can't expect me to remember all of my great grandkids."

"But you know it's two years old."

"The age is nothing. You know how old they are, but any kid under the age of three except for your own is just a kid. You don't really figure out they're a boy or girl till they reach four or five. But if you got eighteen grandkids like me, you sometimes have to wait till their voice changes and if does, it's probably a boy."

Sol's eyebrows went up. "Really? I didn't know that."

"Because you didn't have any kids," Albert pointed out. "If you'd married Norma after high school instead of letting Charlie Mason do it, then you'd know all that shit like me because you'd have eighteen grandkids of your own. Maybe more."

Sol's face went dark and he slunk a bit in his chair. "Norma's got nothing to do with this."

"No shit. That's because she married Charlie Mason instead of you."

Abe leaned forward and stuck his arm across the table between Albert and Sol. "Is there a point to all of this?" he asked. Albert and Sol went silent and looked over. They looked back across the table to each other.

Sol looked at Abe. "A point to what?"

"A point to all of this," Abe said. "You two have been jammering so fast that Fency's getting a sore neck here watching you go back and forth. It's like a freakin' tennis game where you keep banging the ball back and forth but no one's making any points."

Sol leaned back in his chair, arms folded, and stretched his neck to look at the ceiling. He sighed deeply. "The point Abe, is Jerry's grandkids are too old to hang around with him." Sol brought his neck level and twisted it to the right until it cracked and then to the left for another. "So instead of sitting by himself in his big old house, he comes in here every day. And if he sat here everyday just drinking, then he'd be a drunk. This way he's a gambler, which in my opinion is much better than being a drunk."

Fency leaned forward, setting his elbows on the table. "How'd you figure that? Being a gambler is no different than being a drunk. It's just as addictive, and there's lots of people who've lost all their money, their trucks, their houses and their families. Same as drinking. They even got Gamblers Anonymous same as Alcoholics Anonymous."

"Yeah, but Jerry's not one of those gamblers," Sol said.

"He's in here every day."

"Yeah, but if he was drinking here every day spending the same amount he spends on those VLTs, then he'd be an alcoholic. And then he'd stay longer until he'd be shutting this place down. But we all know Jerry comes in here at one o'clock every day and then at four o'clock on the button his watch alarm goes off and he gets up, cashes in any winnings and leaves. Once that alarm goes off that's it for him. He doesn't have another beer, he doesn't talk to anyone, he just leaves.

"Now that means he's a social gambler. But if he drank then he'd be a drunk. You tell me, which one is worse."

Abe drank the rest of his beer and set the empty glass on the table. "Call him what you want Sol, but if these machines weren't in here, Jerry wouldn't be either."

"Yeah, he'd be at home," said Fency.

"Right. And he could play with his grand, no wait, I mean his great grandkids," Abe said. "Since you guys made a big point of pointing that out to us."

"I doubt that," Albert said, making a move to get up. "With Jerry's arthritis, a two year old would probably break him in half."

Sol placed his arm on Albert's shoulder. "Where you going?"

"Over to Elaine's. It's time for supper."

"It's still early. At least finish your beer."

Albert grabbed his glass, gulped it down and slammed the empty glass on the table. "Beer's finished." He stood up.

"You don't want to hear about the IBA and the meeting tonight?" Sol asked. All conversation stopped or drifted off as soon as Sol mentioned the letters IBA.

"Doesn't really affect me does it," Albert said with a noncommittal shrug. The fishermen and the rest of the crowd in the bar started to gather around the table. Albert moved away from the table.

"You guys take it easy," Albert said.

"You too, Albert," said Fency's boy. Abe responded with only a nod.

"You coming to the meeting?" Sol asked. "Starts at eight o'clock."

Albert waved. "If I'm going to be there, I'll be there. Don't worry about me."

"But Albert, you gotta . . . " Sol's voiced trailed away as the people in the crowd demanded to know what was going on with the IBA and whatever meeting he was talking about.

After that, nobody really noticed Albert leaving a few of the company boys gave him goodbye nods, but that was about it. He was too far from the centre of attention. Before he stepped out of the bar, Albert got Jake the daytime bartender to cash in his winnings from the VLTs. The only response he got from Jake was a pair of raised eyebrows. The bartender knew better than to announce who won what from the VLTs, but nobody would have paid any attention to it if he did. They were all still gathered around Sol and soon a bunch of them would run up to the bar and order rounds. When Jake quietly presented the red bills, Albert stuffed them into his pocket. Before he stepped out of the bar, Albert turned and saw that Sol had the attention of the crowd and was starting to tell his story about the IBA.

6

"Let me tell you something about these Hydro guys. They got one of the biggest companies in the province, worth over 40 billion or so, and they're selling power to everybody and their dog south of the border, but they're some of the cheapest bastards out there."

"Even cheaper than Abe?" someone shouted.

"Maybe a little but you guys know how thrifty my brother can be."

"Nothing wrong with being careful with your money," growled Abe. "That's why Hydro's so fucking rich and why you goddamned losers need to worry about the IBA to pay your bills."

"Ahh shut up, Abe. What the hell do you know," someone shouted.

"A lot more than you fucking losers," Abe shouted back.

"You fuckers want to hear the story or what?" Sol asked.

There was more grumbling, but it faded. They weren't too happy about Abe calling them losers but they were willing to let Abe have his way, not because he was right, they'd never admit that, even if he was, but they were more interested to hear Sol tell them about the upcoming IBA payment they were going to get and how he got it for them. So when everybody got their beers squared away and quieted down, Sol began:

"To be completely fair to my brother, Abe's got nothing on these Hydro guys. They're not only cheap but they're stupid cheap. They have so much money kicking around they have no idea what to do with it. Christ, we spent six days negotiating with these bastards trying to nail them down on the IBA. And we worked them hard. We hit them with every single point, made them admit that when they built that dam 30 years ago, they forgot about the people that actually lived on the land they flooded. Sure, they gave us a bunch of crap about economic opportunities and the crap housing they built, but they didn't like being reminded that the only reason they built those crap houses some of you still live in, is that they flooded our traditional homes and slowed down our river so they could make their power. So they had to make a move on the retroactive payments or we'd slow down their regulatory process on the new upgrades.

"That's the big problem with these big companies, they still think we're dumb Indians who don't know shit so we've always got to let them know that we do know shit and if they don't listen to what we say, we're going to fuck 'em up. Companies like Hydro are completely out of it. They still haven't figured out that one day we're going to own this land and they're going to have to deal with us, not because they feel like it but because they have to. And that day's going to come sooner than you expect because those guys in government are getting smart and are starting to figure out that you don't treat us like idiots and that maybe this was our land in the first place.

"So there's a bunch of us in the big Hydro head office, in their big conference meeting room on the top floor of their building in downtown Winnipeg. On one side of this big honking table — and man that thing must have been at least twenty feet long — you got me, our great Chief John B., Larry Mack, Old Dougy Walsh and Albert's girl Jessica. And on the other side of the table is the Hydro crew, most of them not doing much except typing on their laptops or whispering to each other like a bunch of kids. But you also got the big man, Jack Dawson, the king himself, making all the decisions. A couple of Dawson's boys were doing most of the talking, lawyers of some type, but you can tell it's Dawson doing all the work. Every so often he stops everything to say no to this, yes to that, or delegating something to his peons about some figure. Typical hydro shit.

"So there's a bunch of us sitting around this fucking table for six days and we're making some deals here and there. We got them dead to rights on the retro compensation for 30 years ago, but we still had some sticking points on other details. So finally on the last day, we offer them this great deal, meeting them about halfway on where they were last time. Still a damn good deal for us because we got guarantees on jobs, training, community support, and not a bad deal on the cash.

"So after about an hour or so of the Hydro guys whispering and jabbering about nothing, Dawson sits up and says, 'All right, I like the deal where it stands now, everything sits right with me, but I got a little bit of a problem with the cash settlement.'

"'You mean the compensation package,' says Albert's girl Jessica.

"We got Jessica to do most of the talking because she's damn quick on her feet and it really messes up these Hydro boys. She's the only woman in the room and these guys have no idea how to deal with a woman, let alone a big smart Indian girl like Jessica.

" 'This Impact Benefit Agreement is a compensation package for allowing Hydro to use our land,' Jessica says.

"She was doing that kind of stuff all week, correcting Dawson and his boys and reminding them that their dam is on our land and if they don't handle things right, then their dam might become our dam when we work out the land claims with the government. Of course, Dawson isn't picking up on her signals, he just thinks she's doing it to annoy him.

"So Dawson doesn't even look at Jessica, snubbing her like, when he says: 'Whatever you want to call it. This is as far as we're going to go.'

"So like he's seen it in some fucking movie or something, he writes a figure on a piece of paper and slides it across the table to us. It sits there for a second or two, until Jessica reaches out and picks it up. All of a sudden, she looks all confused, giving Dawson this look like he's some sort of crazy nut.

" 'Are you serious with this?' she asks Dawson, and the old bastard doesn't say anything. He just nods his head, still not looking at her, but nodding his head. Of course the rest of us are all keen to know what Dawson's written that makes Jessica look at him so funny. I'm thinking he's written zero or something stupid like that as a joke. Wouldn't put it past Dawson or any of his boys to do something like that. So Larry Mack, who's sitting next to Jessica, picks it up and looks at it. Larry's not really the big money-man on the committee, he's more of job security guy, making sure you guys get plenty of work and training out of this thing, but you can tell he's not happy with the figure on the paper. He passes it down the line and it just happens that I'm at the other end so that by the time the paper reaches me, everybody's gotten real cold because of the number on the sheet. It messes everything up so much that John B., who we told to keep his mouth shut on this whole deal until the end, starts talking to Dawson.

"'But that's only a ten-thousand-dollar difference, Jack. You can't be serious?'

"I look at the paper and see that he's right. The bastard's figure is only 10,000 bucks less than our offer. It's fucking peanuts and Dawson knows it too, but he don't move, he just sits there in his blue Tory suit saying, 'That's my final offer on this thing. We can't afford to go any further.'

"I thought John B. and Jessica were going to go through the roof. And you know, I wouldn't blame them 'cause it was a cheapshot offer. Jessica must have cleared her confusion because the next thing you know, she's jumping out of her chair banging on the table.

"'You can't be serious with this offer! You can't be! We offer you a good solid deal and you come back with this piece of crap! After all this time we've spent talking and building some kind of trust you pull this kind of stunt.'

"Albert's girl would have reached across the table to strangle that old bastard for such a cheapshot move, but Larry Mack put a hand on her arm. She backed down a bit, but she kept at them.

"'This is typical Hydro bullshit,' she said. 'You talk a good game with your billion-dollar PR department sending out newsletters and press releases about putting the past behind you and wanting to work as partners with our people, but it's the same old-fashioned Hydro from twenty years ago. You still think you're doing us a favour by including us in this negotiation, don't you. You guys still don't get it. Are you that stupid that — '

"One of the Hydro boys spoke up to defend his company. 'There's no need for personal insults here.'

"Man, I thought Jessica was going to explode when she heard that; she banged her hand on the table so hard that she knocked over a couple of water glasses. Larry Mack had to quickly push his chair back so he wouldn't get wet.

"'Insult! Insult!' she shouted, and I thought the Hydro flake who spoke up was going to have a heart attack, he looked so scared. The rest of the Hydro boys looked the same way, like they just wanted out of the room away from the big scary squaw. But Jack Dawson didn't flinch. He kept looking at John B. as if Jessica wasn't even there. Jessica must've noticed that too because she just took a deep breath and calmed herself. She sat back down in her chair and pointed at the piece of paper.

"'That,' she said, 'is an insult. An insult to every one of us sitting on this side of the table and to every single person in our community. That, is an insult to our people.'

"'I'm sorry you feel that way,' Dawson said. 'But my hands are tied in this matter. Our shareholders have told

71

us that we must keep these things to a minimum and this is as far as I'm willing to go.'

"'What a load of crap,' says Old Dougy Walsh, but John B. sitting next to him holds up his hand to shut him up.

"'Surely Hydro can afford to make up the difference,' John B. says like the diplomat he is. 'It's only $10,000.'

"But Jack Dawson wasn't moving and I knew why he wasn't. It had nothing to do with the money, Christ, $10,000 is nothing to that old bastard; a couple of those laptops his lackeys were working on were worth more than that ten grand. The old guy just wanted to make a point. He knew we kicked his ass on the retro payment on the original construction and he was pissed about it so he thought he'd give us one more shot just to make him feel good before he went home that night. He needed something so he could tell his other conglomo buddies that he still had the balls to stick it to us fucking Indians one last time before he retired. I could tell from the looks on the faces of his peons that this is just what he wanted to do. He wanted to fuck us up one final time and it was working. He pretty much had everybody on our side of the table so messed up about the deal that a few of them were probably even willing to walk out of the room. And then he could say that he made us a decent offer — even minus the ten grand it was a good offer — but he could say we were unwilling to meet him halfway. That old bastard had nothing to lose.

"But before anybody walked out of the room and before Dawson got too smug, I cleared my throat and told the Hydro boys that we'd take their deal. Of course everybody looked at me like I was fucked in the head, but I looked at John B. 'We've been working this deal for months, I myself haven't slept more than five hours in the last few days and since we're this close, we should finish up this thing and take the offer.'

"Jessica looked like she wanted to string me up with Dawson. 'You can't be serious about this, Sol. This offer, although close to what we want, should be considered an insult. And we should respond in kind.'

"'I'm not happy about it either, Jessica. I don't believe that Mr. Dawson is being completely forward with us about the concerns of his shareholders and his hands being tied, but I still think we should accept this deal. We'll just waste valuable time going back and forth when it's obvious that Mr. Dawson has no plans to move any closer to us. We should just accept the deal and sign this IBA today. Our people will be happy with it, and that's the important thing.'

"I also gave Jessica a little wink to let her know that I understood what she meant, but I had something else in mind and not to worry. And then I went a little philosophical, just in case she didn't get my meaning. 'The Creator tells us that everything we do is connected to everything else and in the end, all things will work themselves out in some way or another. We should accept Hydro's deal and let things work out on their own.'

"The Hydro boys thought that was great, especially my bit about the Creator. Great PR for them to have me say something like that. They thought that we were being good Indians for going along with their plan. And Jack Dawson had this big smile on his face, like he just broke up the Beatles or something like that, but he had no idea what was going on. He thought he made a good deal and when John B. finally agreed with me and decided to go ahead and accept the deal, Dawson's smile got even bigger. All the Hydro folks started applauding when we accepted.

"'This is a great day,' Dawson said. 'A great move forward for our two peoples. A great day for celebration. The Creator smiles upon our two peoples.'

"Don't get me wrong, this was a good deal, we got pretty much everything we wanted, all the retro cash, which we never thought we'd get, and enough job security and training for everyone in the fucking room, but Dawson showed us what kind of guy he was with that cheapshot at the end. He showed me, everybody at that table and the rest of you guys here that he didn't give a shit about you. To him, we're still just a bunch of dumb Indians and he wanted to show us just that. Which is why I said earlier that these Hydro guys may be cheap, but they're stupid cheap. Dawson got so excited about the deal that after the signing, he invited all of us out for drinks and dinner at the hotel where we were all staying.

"'We've all worked hard for this new day. Damn fucking hard,' he said. 'God knows I could use a bit of a party. So name your poison because I'm buying.'

"So the bunch of us head down to the hotel restaurant and bar and let me tell you, it's no dive. This is one of the places where they got the finest of everything, champagne, brandy, 24-year-old scotch, lobster, steaks, you name it. So when we walked in, Dawson started throwing his weight around and got the place to set up a private area in the back. We had a few drinks, Dawson ordered some bottles of champagne, but after a bit, Old Dougy got up to leave.

"'Where the hell are you going?' Dawson asked. 'The party's just started.'

"'I got my wife and boys up at the room,' Dougy said.

"'Bring them down. Let 'em join the celebration,' Dawson said.

"'You sure?'

"Dawson probably thought that Dougy has a wife and a couple of little tykes but he doesn't realize that his boys have also brought their wives and kids.

"'Why the hell not. Bring the whole family,'" Dawson said.

"I slapped an arm around Dawson like I was his best buddy in the world. 'Sure Dougy, bring the whole family down. It's a party.' So Dougy shrugs and heads out to get his family.

"Dawson then said, 'If the rest of you guys have family with you, bringthem down to join the party.' So Larry Mack headed out to get his wife and Jessica just got up to go to the bathroom. With everybody moving around, Dawson figured it was a good time to sneak out. He'd have a few toasts with us, but he wasn't going to hang around all night with a bunch of Indians. He wanted to get to his Tory committee or CEO clubhouse to gloat about how he stuck it to us. So he shook my hand, and John B.'s too, congratulating us for our cool heads. And before he left, he made a big point of telling the restaurant manager that he'd take care of the bill.

"So after Dawson left, everybody started to have a pretty good time. We worked hard you know and it was good to relax after. Jessica came back and said that when she went to her room, she ran into Brian's uncle, you know, the bishop, and he's on some sort of bishop retreat in town.

"'Bring him along,' I told her.

"'What? Are you crazy?'

"'Why not? He's family. And the rest of his buddies are spiritual leaders. I don't think Jack Dawson would mind if we include our spiritual advisors in our little celebration. I gave her a little wink and the next thing you know, she's got a big smile on her face. She punched me hard on the arm.

"'You're a real son of a bitch, Sol Jacks. Jack Dawson's going to have a heart attack.'

"'Like I said, the Creator tells us that everything we do is connected.'

"'The Creator tells me that you're a son of a bitch and that I should be thankful that you're on our side.'

"'Each of us gets a different message from the Creator. Go get your uncle and we'll see what he says.'

"So she headed out and Larry Mack's wife remembered that they got some cousins in town. John B. remembered that he got a couple cousins, too. So they gave 'em a call and they all came down. Jessica brought Brian's uncle and the rest of the bishops to the show. There were only six of them but I tell you those bishops sure can pack away the booze and the eats. And with everybody's family and shit, we got about 40 Cree and their friends hanging around, having the time of their lives. And we weren't ordering rum and cokes you know, like we were in Norway House or something. We were in the big city so we went for the 24-year-old scotch, more bottles of champagne, and all the steak and lobster with all the trimmings.

"Fuck, I don't know what time we finished that night or how much we drank; I was just lucky I found my bed. But the next morning, or it might have been afternoon, I really can't remember the time, my phone started ringing. It rang and rang and I figured if I let it go, it would stop. And it did, but only for a second. It started ringing and ringing again, so I figured, what the fuck, I'll answer it. You'll never believe it but it was old Jack Dawson giving me a wake-up call.

"'Hey Jack. How's it hanging?' I asked him.

"For a second or too there was nothing but heavy breathing. But then Jack Dawson said, 'What the hell did you guys do last night?'

"'Hell Jack, we were celebrating like you told us to. You should have hung around longer; it was a hell of a party. On behalf of the members of the Grand Rapids Cree people, I'd like to thank you for your hospitality.'

"'Do you have any idea how much the bill was?'

"'Can't say I do. I wasn't paying. We told the manager to include a good tip because the service was excellent. You got some nice food-service people in your city. They really know how to treat a guest. They also had these comment cards so you can tell the hotel how the service was, so a bunch of us wrote some nice things about — '

"'You bastards spent over $20,000 last night. $20,000! On my expense account! You know how that's going to look when I have to explain to the board of directors why I spent $20,000! In one night! Do you have any idea what that means!?'

"The old bastard yelled some more but I just waited and picked my nose until he finished. And then I said with a whistle, '$20,000. If my arithmetic is still good, that's two times $10,000. Go figure.'

"There was silence on the phone for a bit while Dawson finally figured things out. It took him so long to answer, I thought he was gone and was ready to hang up and go back to sleep. But finally, he said, 'You are some son of a bitch, Sol Jacks. Anybody ever tell you that? You. Are. A. Goddamned. Son. Of. A. Bitch!'

"'Right back at you, Dawson,' I told him. 'Right back at you.'

"And then I hung up and went back to sleep."

7

When Albert left the Grand Rapids bar with his winnings in his pocket, the air was cool and a light wind blew over the trees. He briefly squinted up at the sky. Dark puffs of clouds, billowing upwards and drifting from the west, hung in the sky with the sun peeking in and out every few minutes. Over the lake to the northeast, these clouds would gather together like old family members at a reunion before moving off as a group over the lake, a threatening grey scale of constant yet unseen growth.

Albert reached the edge of the parking lot, shuffled down the well-worn path through the ditch and up to the road that came off the highway and led traffic towards the centre of the Reserve and then further on to the dam and the Cedar Lake forebay area. Before crossing the road, Albert checked to the left, then the right just in time to see a small blue pickup pull off the highway onto the road. The truck, with its white topper on the box, beeped once and stopped in front of him. The driver rolled down his window and waved. "Hey Albert. How's it going?"

Albert nodded in response and walked up to the truck. "Good Bud. How's it going with you?" He leaned his elbow against the hood near the bottom of the windshield.

"Can't complain, can't complain," Bud said, nodding quickly. He slipped the gearshift into park. Bud was a thick, stocky man with a pudgy face and black curly hair cut close to his head. His eyebrows were thick and would have made one line across his brow except for a distinct lack of hair above his nose, as if he regularly shaved that spot. His eyes were thin slits that were barely open and his nose hung low, flat and slightly off-centre. A neatly trimmed handlebar mustache sat over his mouth, making up for his lack of lips. His face ended in a round knobby chin that drew attention away from the small mounds of flesh that hung off his neck. Bud looked up at the sky and the developing clouds over the lake. "Looks like rain though."

Albert looked up and nodded. "Probably going to storm tonight."

"You think so? Those clouds look like they're heading to the east."

"They'll be back," Albert said quietly. "They'll bunch up over the lake, bounce around Long Point for a bit and then when it gets cooler later tonight, they'll come booshing in."

"Big one, you guess?"

Albert nodded. "Probably. Depends on how long it stays out there."

"Then I better close the windows before I go to bed tonight."

"Be a good idea. Bring the dogs in too."

Bud's face frowned with concern. "That bad?" he asked.

Albert nodded. "Check the trees," he said, pointing to the clump of forest behind the Esso station across the road. Bud ducked into the truck and peered through the windshield. Bud shrugged, so Albert explained. "Already they're starting to sway and the storm's still a few hours away."

Bud shook his head and looked back at Albert. "Guess I'll have to put out the cat then, eh Albert?" he said with a smile.

Albert's eyes narrowed and blinked in confusion. "Didn't know you had a cat, Bud? I thought Jodi was allergic?"

Bud laughed for a few seconds. "We don't have a cat." Albert didn't laugh with him, so Bud explained further. "It was a joke."

Albert rubbed his chin with the palm of his hand. "I don't get it."

"You remember Old Lady Sinclair," Bud waved his hand, gesturing back with his thumb, "used to live in that green trailer where Danny Morgan and his kids live now."

"Yeah, Mabel Sinclair. Nice lady," Albert said. "Didn't like her dogs though, barking all the time."

"Yeah, they were noisy little shits weren't they?"

"Yeah, they were," Albert nodded. "Died a few years ago didn't she?"

"Old Lady Sinclair? 'Bout seven years ago."

"That long ago?"

"Yep. She got cancer of the pancreas or the stomach, something like that. She weighed about 70 pounds when she died. Her son Owen asked me to be a pallbearer, and man you know what that's like. It's a heavy job, feels like you're going to break a shoulder lifting one of those coffins, but since we were neighbours, what could I say? I couldn't say no, you know what I mean."

"Not when her son's asking you, you can't."

"That's right. When someone dies you don't offer to be a pallbearer, but when they ask you to do it, you can't refuse them."

"I've been there myself."

"Right, then you know what I'm talking about. So I told Mabel's son Owen that yeah, since we were neighbours, I'd be one of the pallbearers," Bud said. "And I was expecting to break a hip 'cause old Mabel died in the winter and they didn't get the sidewalk in front of the church cleared that good because we got a lot of snow that winter. Man, that was a bad year for snow. But you wouldn't believe how light that coffin was. It felt like we were carrying a box of air, the six of us. I was so tempted to shake the coffin, just a little bit, so I could hear something rattle so I'd believe that she was in there, but I didn't think they'd appreciate it."

Albert chuckled. "Probably not."

"Yeah, Mabel, she was a nice old lady, except for her dogs and all. And so she'd get all weird and crazy whenever there was a thunderstorm. She'd get fidgety and nervous like some kind of scared mouse and bang on our door, reminding us not to use the phone and to turn off the TV, 'cause the lightning could come through the phone and electrocute you if you were talking to someone. Or it would come into the TV line and your set would explode or catch on fire." Bud raised his voice to a gravelly falsetto. "Don't you laugh at me Duncan Ray Spencer," he dropped his voice, "she always called me that when she was mad," raised it again to falsetto, "don't you laugh at me. I've seen it happen when they first came out. Murray Johnson left his TV on during a thunderstorm and the damn thing exploded on him. Nearly set the house on fire, so don't laugh at me." He laughed and then continued in his own voice. "What a crazy lady she was sometimes. And every time, even though she knew we never had one, even before we had Jodi and her allergies, she'd tell us to put our cat out 'cause it wasn't a good idea to have a cat in the house when there was a storm."

"I never heard that one," Albert said. "Why'd you have to put the cat out in a thunderstorm? Make more sense to bring the poor thing in."

Bud shrugged and spit onto the road. "Beats me. Something about lightning being attracted to cats," she said. "I could never figure out what she was talking about sometimes. She said something in their fur or because they're always cleaning themselves, creates a lot of static electricity and that makes them a perfect lightning rod."

Albert shook his head. "Doesn't make sense. If you put a cat out in a thunderstorm, the only thing it's going to do is climb underneath the house or the steps to stay dry so what's the point of putting it out. If a cat's some type of lightning rod, then the lightning's still going to hit the house to get to the cat."

"That's exactly what I figured. I don't know where these old people get their ideas."

"Old people are like that," Albert said. "When they finally got running water up in my mom's house in Norway House, she'd always go outside and use the old outhouse when there was a storm 'cause she said the water from the toilet would attract lightning. I remember my brother Larry shouting at her that going outside in the trees to use the outhouse was worse than using the bathroom but she wouldn't listen. She'd never come within ten feet of the bathroom when there was a storm."

"Yeah those old people had some crazy ideas," Bud said.

"You're right," replied Albert. And then there were several seconds of silence. Albert stared up at the clouds and Bud looked down the road ahead of him.

Bud sat up quickly and slapped the side of his truck. "Hey! You going to the meeting tonight?"

"What meeting?"

"You know, the IBA meeting. At the community hall."

"You heard about the meeting already? Sol Jacks was just telling everybody about it. How'd you hear about it?"

"Shit, Albert. The whole town's talking about it. I was delivering some paper over at the band office this morning and I could hear Joe B. in his office talking to someone about it. The way he was strutting around and going on about the IBA with Hydro it sounded like he just got us self-government or something. Even so, still sounds like a good deal. Plenty of guaranteed jobs for everybody, 'specially you."

"Oh yeah. Think they'd hire me?"

Bud's eyes opened wide with surprise. "Shit! You Albert? They'd hire you on the spot. You put how many years on that dam while they were building it? Eight? Ten?"

"Twelve," Albert said, quietly. "Started when there was no dam and got laid off when we finally completed the project."

Bud slapped the side of his truck twice and pointed a finger at Albert. "Well, there you go, Albert. You're probably the kind of guy they're looking for. They'd probably make you a supervisor or something with all you know about the place."

"I don't know." Albert scratched his chin and then moved up to his hair. Flecks of dirt and sand fell off. "That was a long time ago. If they think I would have made a good supervisor, why'd they lay me off when they finished the damn thing?"

"They laid everybody off and brought in all these experts from Winnipeg to run things for them. That's the way Hydro used to work with all their dams. Get all the locals to build them and then lay them off when everything's done and bring in experts from somewhere else to run things. Maybe keep one or two local guys around to clean up the place to look good."

"Yeah, but I think I might be a little too old for what they're looking for." More flecks of dirt and sand fell from Albert's hair.

"Jesus you're barely 60 yet, so you got nothing to worry about. Besides, everybody knows if you need someone to work hard, they call you."

Albert shrugged. "Yeah, but most of these Manitoba Hydro guys won't know me."

"Jesus, Albert!" Bud exclaimed. "What about Brian?"

"Brian?"

"Jessie's guy."

"Oh him. Yeah, he knows me."

"He's your son-in-law, eh! Of course he knows you. With him in your corner, you'll probably be one of the first ones hired."

"I don't know about that. He keeps telling me I should get my treaty number."

"You should. It's what I'm counting on. Because of the IBA, they have to hire a good chunk of us and I've already got my application in. You should do the same once you get a treaty number."

"Yeah. I've been thinking about that," Albert said. "Jessie gave me a form a few months ago and I was planning to fill it out but I put it in a drawer someplace."

"Don't worry about it then Albert, just go to the meeting." Bud brought his hands into the truck and placed them on the steering wheel.

"I don't know," Albert said, stepping away from the truck.

Bud slipped the truck into drive and it jerked forward slightly. "Listen, Albert. I gotta get supper ready for Gerri and the kids, but later, since you're without any wheels, I'll come by and pick you up."

"You don't have to do that."

Bud waved him away. "Fuck, Albert. I'm just down the street so I'll have to pass by your house on the way to the community centre anyways, so I'll beep you and give you a ride. Seven all right?"

Albert nodded. "Okay I'll see you then," Bud said and pulled away, leaving a cloud of dust. Albert waved, stepped through the cloud and headed towards the Esso station.

8

The Esso station just across from the bar had four pumps, two regular, one premium, and one diesel, and near the back, the regulation 75 metres from the building, a propane tank and pump. The main building was split in two with the convenience store on one side and the restaurant on the other, separated by a hallway with a pay phone and the entrances to the men's and women's washrooms.

A semi-trailer truck — a black Kenworth cab covered in a thin layer of road dust and dead flies, and a silver unlabelled refrigeration trailer unit producing a light mosquito swarm buzz — sat off to the side of the parking lot. The driver was either sleeping in his cab or eating lunch in the restaurant. Since Winnipeg and the Trans-Canada was only five hours away, trucks rarely stopped on their way north, so Albert figured the driver was taking a quick break in the restaurant; why sleep in Grand Rapids, when Winnipeg, probably the driver's home, was just down the road.

At the pumps there was only one vehicle, a camper-ized van, unblemished by road dust and with just a thin layer of dead bugs on the front windshield. The van featured several additions that Albert could recognize: a three-foot-wide satellite dish, folded down on the roof like some type of space module device, and a canopy, rolled up like a giant window blind over the main door. But it was what the motorhome was hauling that grabbed Albert's attention. Even though it was hidden underneath a grey tarp tightly held by countless bungee cords, Albert knew the boat was something special. He stared at its sleek, streamlined form, imagining various joys beneath the wrapping:

Seats, not just one for the driver but enough for several passengers. Proper seats, cushioned, with backs and armrests that you could adjust, like office chairs;

A steering wheel, not a plastic rod attached to the engine to control the direction of the boat;

Electric start, probably with some type of fuel injection system instead of a manual choke, a throttle control for a variety of speeds up to a top speed that would probably take you across the lake in an hour to a low idle that would barely make a ripple in the water.

Albert walked along the side of the boat, running his hands along the tarp, trying to feel the colour underneath. Blue trim, he hoped, not some bright, modern colour that some boaters seemed to be taken with, and a gleaming white fibreglass hull, clean and unmarked by harsh weeds and rocks. Even the engine was wrapped in its own tarp, but Albert could tell that underneath, it was a monster. 150 or 200 horsepower in that confined space of a plastic covering, powerful enough to pull a hockey team of water skiers and, if they wanted to come along, their fans. Albert reached out to touch the engine, but for some reason didn't want to bring his hand close enough. He held it there, knowing that this engine, even from a 100 yards away, would make his little Lund twirl and dance in its wake.

"She's a beaut, isn't she?" a voice said.

Albert continued looking at the boat but peripherally could see a tall man dressed in various shades of khaki green and carrying a plastic bag of packages and glass approach him.

"She is," Albert said. "She truly is."

"Evinrude 175," the man said, now standing next to Albert. "Goes like stink. She'll take you where you want to go and back so fast and so smooth you'd think you were riding on glass."

Albert looked at the man. He was about three inches taller than Albert and maybe 50 pounds lighter. His clothing, a thick cotton shirt covered by a heavy vest with various sized pockets everywhere, some zippered, some buttoned, others opened; a matching pair of pants with pockets up and down the legs, and a pair of workboots that looked too clean, flexible and expensive to be real workboots. And every piece, newly bought, with their folding creases and department store crispness still attached. The man also wore a khaki ballcap that had no logo, no word nor any type of marking on the front. He wore a light pair of wire-rimmed glasses, and although his pale face lacked many of the outdoor wrinkles that Albert's held, there were still some down by the mouth and around the eyes. There was also a type of look in the man's eyes that made Albert a little uncomfortable. This man, Albert knew, was some type of boss, a controller of people, but not like Barings.

Though Barings was the scaleman for the company and completely responsible for how much you got paid for your fish every day, you never sensed a difference in power with Barings, just annoyance. But this guy had a Jerry Harrison, Albert's boss on his first job on the Keweetan, thing about him. It was "I'm your fucking boss, you know it and I know it so don't you fuck up or I'll fucking kill you" kind of thing. But this guy also had a friendly smile and a relaxed attitude, things Harrison never possessed. And besides, Jerry Harrison wouldn't talk to you about his new boat, firstly, 'cause he would have never bought one and if it didn't have anything to do with the job, he wanted nothing to do with you or anybody for that matter.

"She looks like it," Albert said.

"Want to see it?" the guy said, reaching up to loosen the tarp.

But Albert shook his head. "Don't worry about it."

"You sure?" the guy said. "It's no trouble."

"I can picture it from here," Albert said with a wave.

The guy pulled his hand down and chuckled. "Guess you're right. How could you miss? Big fancy camper van pulls in, with a satellite dish and all the trimmings, and towing a monster of a boat. Bet the whole town saw me coming in."

"Probably, but usually we're too polite to say anything about it."

The guy chuckled again and then stuck out his hand. "Neely, Ted Neely."

Albert took the hand and shook it. It was a firm grip, tight and practised, just like the bosses at Hydro when they visited the dam during and after construction. "Albert Apetagon," he said.

Neely gestured with his head to the surrounding trees. "You live 'round here long?"

"More than 40 years."

Neely whistled through his teeth. "Any good fishing 'round here?"

"Lots of fishing around here. Just depends on what kind you're looking for."

"Oh, nothing too fancy for me, but you wouldn't know that from all the stuff I brought," Neely said. "I just like to sit in my boat out on some lake and set up my rod and stick out my line. Right now I don't really care if I catch anything, I just like to relax. Took an early retirement, was either that or they lay me off so I cashed in my stock and took the money and ran, so to speak. Best move I ever made." Albert listened but couldn't think of anything in response so he didn't reply. Neely seemed to notice so he paused for a couple of seconds and then asked Albert a question.

"So what do you, Albert?"

Albert smiled. "I'm a fisherman," he said.

Neely blinked several times. "A fisherman? You mean a guide?"

He shook his head. "Commercial fisherman."

"Really?" Neely's eyes grew wide. "You mean they still have commercial fishing up here? That's amazing." Neely's face suddenly turned red and he quickly looked away. "Jesus, what a dope I am. Here I am talking 'bout sitting on my boat relaxing and it's probably what you do every day. I figure it's not as relaxing for you."

"It can be at times, but it's still a job."

"At least you get to work someplace nice. Got yourself a beautiful country here. Trees, lakes, rivers, no big cities for hundreds of miles. Must be nice." Albert nodded, not saying anything. "'Course you've probably heard that hundreds of times . . . " Neely's voice trailed off and the wind whistled to the silence they created. Albert checked the sky, watching the clouds gather above, and then moved his gaze to watch an old pickup move north along the highway. His gaze drifted back and he made eye contact with Neely. There seemed to be a flash of recognition, as if they each knew something about the other but were unwilling to share it.

Neely looked away first. "Good to meet you Albert," he said, sticking out his right hand. Albert gripped it, and they both gave a long squeeze, not too hard, but tight enough to show each other they were there.

"You enjoy your fishing," Albert said.

Neely nodded. "You too."

And then they separated and turned away. Albert walked towards the Esso, but stopped when he heard the engine of Neely's rig start up. He walked over to the rig and tapped on the passenger window. It slid down on its own power and Neely looked over, a questioning yet hard look on his face. "Something I can do for you Albert? I really need to get going. I don't want be on the highway during the dark."

Albert ignored the annoyed tone in Neely's voice. "Fishing around Norway House and Cross Lake is pretty good."

Neely's face softened instantly. "Really? How good?"

"I grew up there," Albert said, gesturing northward with his head and pursing his lips.

Neely's eyes went wide for a second, but then returned to normal. "That good?"

Albert nodded. "Just follow this main highway north till you can't go any farther, make a right on number 6 and then make another right on the Norway House turnoff. It's a gravel road after that, so most don't like to make the trip. When you get to the ferry, tell Joel that Albert Apetagon in Grand Rapids told you that there was some nice fishing nearby. He'll fill you in on the rest."

Neely smiled. "I really appreciate that Albert. Is there any way I can repay you?" He started to move his hand to his pocket but then pulled it back.

Albert shook his head. "You just have a nice time fishing," he said, and then stepped back. Neely looked at him for a second and then the window slid up to close. He put the rig in gear, gave Albert a final wave and then pulled out. Albert watched the back of the boat with the huge engine until it disappeared around the curve.

TWO YEARS AGO

Their footsteps creaked across the old, worn wood of the company's pier and despite Albert's increasing fatigue, they walked in sync, two pairs of feet sounding like one. When they arrived at the spot where the company boat was parked, they stopped and then Fency's boy quickly turned to face Albert, crossing his arms in front of his chest to keep his grip on the blanket. He looked down on the body and froze for a second. A look of fear and dismay came over his face. Tears welled up in his eyes and he looked up at Albert. Albert nodded once and said softly, "If you want I'll call Sol and we can take it from here."

The boy stared down at his father's body for a couple more seconds, sniffed once and shook his head. "I'm okay. Let's get him on the boat."

As if choreographed, they each put one foot on the gunnel; the boat dipped slightly in the water, but they adjusted their weight to compensate. They swung the load over the rail and stepped up, briefly balanced on the gunne, and then moved onto the deck. The boat rocked back and forth as they set down the load. Albert's arms responded by drifting upward on their own.

"I'll cover him up," Albert said. "Don't want him to get cold." He bent down and folded the exposed ends of the blanket over the body. He lifted up the feet and tucked the ends underneath. He repeated the same gesture with the upper body, but kept the head exposed. He brushed off the blanket to smooth out the wrinkles. Sol Jacks and Barings came from the weighing area to the boat.

Barings laid a hand on the boy's shoulder. "It's better if you go," he whispered. "No need for you to hang around here anymore."

Light flared from a match as Sol sparked a cigarette. He extinguished the match with a quick flick of his wrist and tossed it into the water. "Yeah, it's better if you go and let them handle things from here," Sol said. Smoke escaped from his mouth as he spoke.

"I'm going out," Fency's boy said, nodding towards the lake.

"You sure? You don't have to stay 'cause I don't want to get you into more trouble," Albert said. "I appreciate you helping me carrying the body down, but we should handle it from here. Sol will take you home, won't you Sol."

Sol nodded, but the boy waved the suggestion away. "I'll get the ropes," he said. He jumped off the boat onto the pier and it swayed underneath him.

"What 'bout you Barings? You coming?" Sol asked.

"With you? You staying here aren't you?"

"Boat's pretty crowded now that the boy's going along."

"So."

Sol took a nervous puff of his smoke. "So I figured you might want to come with me," he said.

"What the hell gave you that idea?"

Sol shrugged but said nothing. Albert climbed out of the boat and stood next to Barings. He whispered, "I'm going to ask you to leave, Barings. It's not necessary for you to go. You'll only get in bigger trouble if there's any problem."

"It's my boat," Barings declared.

"It's the company boat," Sol said quietly.

Barings stared at Sol for several seconds and then took one step forward. The anger seethed in his eyes, but the rest of his body was calm. "I'm the company in this town so that makes it my boat. Without it, none of this would be happening."

Sol took a step back, his hands raised in appeasement. "Take it easy Barings. No need — "

Barings cut him off. "You fuckin' asshole, Jacks. You really piss me off. I fished on this lake with you independents for over ten years and just because I decide to pack it in for something a little more relaxing at my age, you treat me like an outcast. But when you need something from good old Barings, I'm your best friend again, until of course, you don't get the right price for your fish, or you bring in a bad load, then it's all —"

Albert placed his hand on Barings' shoulder, stopping the tirade. "We're just looking out for you Barings," Albert said, his voice serene and smooth. "You're in enough trouble already and we, I mean I, figured that if you stayed here, you could say you knew nothing and that the boat was stolen, if anything happened."

Barings twisted away. "You piss me off too with this, Albert. You think you were Fency's only friend, just

because you fished a few years longer together than I
did."

"That's not it Barings."

"We worked for two years on the Keweetan till you
came along, Albert. Two years loading and unloading
that barge while Jerry Harrison screamed his fucking
lungs out at us. Two years before you, Albert. Two years.
That makes him just as important a friend to me than
to you."

"I never said you weren't his friend, Barings."

"Jesus Christ!" Fency's boy shouted, surprising
everyone. "This is my old man here so show some
respect and stop bickering!" Albert, Barings and Sol
watched in silence as the younger man finished untying
the bowlines and tossed the ropes on the deck. He
pushed between Albert and Barings and climbed into
the boat. He went over to the steering wheel and started
the engine, a roar in the silence and a cloud of black
diesel blew out of the exhaust. In seconds the engine
pounded with healthy chugs. The boy walked to the
centre of the boat and stood with his hands on his hips.
He gave his head a quick upward flick and pursed his
lips towards Albert. "Me and Albert will take Dad out.
I'm sorry Barings, I appreciate you letting us use the
boat but that's the way it's going to be."

Barings began to speak but the boy cut him off. "I
know you were his friend for a long time Barings and
he knows it too. He didn't mind when you went over to
the company. He figured it was the best thing for you,
but the fact is Dad asked Albert to do this for him. And
even though this is your boat, with Dad aboard there's

only room for one more and I know you wouldn't mind if I went along."

Barings said nothing for several seconds and then finally nodded. "At least I can say goodbye to him then."

"Nobody's stopping you from doing that," the boy said, and he and Albert stepped aside. Barings looked like he was carrying a heavy load on his back as he slowly lowered himself to his knees. He bent forward until he was a few inches away from the face and whispered something. He nodded as if listening and then kissed the forehead. He gave the body a friendly slap. He started to push himself up but stumbled. One of his arms reached out for balance and Albert grabbed it to steady him. The two men looked at each other for several seconds before Barings, with Albert's help, pulled himself to feet. "Thanks Albert," he said. Albert nodded, gave Barings's arm a quick squeeze and then let go. Barings wiped some tears from his eyes and slowly stepped out of the boat to stand on the pier next to Sol. Albert climbed aboard just as the boat jerked away from the pier.

"You guys be careful," Sol said. "It's pretty dark out there."

"We'll be alright," Albert answered back. "Not as if we haven't been on the lake at night."

"Yeah but you haven't —" Sol began to say but then changed his mind. "Just take it easy out there."

Albert nodded and the boy steered the boat towards the lake. The company boat pushed through the darkness, slicing an invisible line through the black surface. Sol and Barings watched them disappear into the darkness and then watched the noise of the engine.

When it faded, slipping behind the point, they watched the silence. Finally, Sol said, "Buy you a beer?"

Barings nodded. "Several," he said, and they turned and walked back up the pier towards the town.

NORWAY HOUSE

1

The highway that ran north from Grand Rapids was a shiny new blacktop sliced in half by a bright yellow stream of dotted lines and protected on both sides by shoulders at least eight feet wide. A strip about 300 metres wide had been sliced through the forest to make room for the highway and to act as a utility corridor. Two sets of power lines ran parallel with the highway, one on each side of the road with ten lines in each set. Every half kilometre or so, the metal skeletons of tall giants stood steadfast and unmoving, arms raised and fingers spread to support the wires that carried Hydro's electricity from the countless dams in the north to the millions of users in the south. Traffic on the road was relatively light: a few campers and boats heading north to sport-fishing spots and eighteen-wheelers going north to Flin Flon, Thompson, and the Pas or south to Winnipeg.

Because of the light traffic and the warmth of the air, Sol drove with one arm draped on the open window, the other hand casually gripping the wheel. A light breeze blew from the east off the lake that at this point was hidden behind the heavy muskeg and the thick forest. The wind made the trees waver softly and produced a gentle hum from the power lines, but Sol's truck barely rattled as it traveled down the road. Albert sat on the passenger side in the same manner as Sol, but his inside hand gripped a can of beer. Between Sol and Albert was Bud Riley, his short legs spread wide to straddle the drive-train hump. Bud's stocky body took up as much space as he could and his hands constantly played with his neatly trimmed handlebar mustache. Bud spoke with a native accent, the words blurring and slurring slightly and then inflecting at the end of each sentence as if he was asking a question. "Hey Albert, how come we're taking the highway and not the lake? It's gotta be at least six hours by road and only two by boat, eh."

"It's a new highway," Albert answered, keeping his eyes forward.

"Albert and me spent two years building this new road so we figured for this trip we'd see how it turned out," Sol said. He brought his outside arm in and leaned forward on the steering wheel with his elbows. He turned and looked over to Albert. "What do you think, Albert? Did we do a good job or what?"

Albert coughed slightly. "Better than most highways in this goddamn province. At least they put a shoulder on this one."

"Won't last, though," said Sol.

"I give it two, three years. Maybe four at the most," Bud said.

"Probably less," said Albert. "It'll be fine till winter and then when the frost breaks, it'll eat this highway alive. And then in the summer the muskeg will start seeping in and with the big rigs running back and forth to Winnipeg, it'll soon be a piece of shit. Like every other fucking crap highway in this province."

"All the work you and Sol did gone to waste, eh Albert?"

"Paid us well for two years," Sol said.

"Paid us mighty well," Albert added. "And then maybe ten years from now, they might pay you well Bud."

"Sure hope it's sooner, you know," Bud said. "Not much happening in town and with them still talking about the upgrading of the dam, who knows when a good job will come up. Two years, they say, before they start the project. Two years before they start hiring."

"Think you'll get on?" Sol asked.

Bud laughed and slapped Sol on the shoulder. "Well shit, you know that better than me Sol, you being on the IBA committee and all. I just know that if my welding ticket don't get me in, then it's up to Sol and his committee from the band to fight for my aboriginal rights. Won't help you Albert, you being a white man and all." He laughed and dug an elbow into Albert's ribs.

Albert smiled and chuckled. "I don't know about that. They gotta hire a few white men for the project so I might as well be the token one."

"That's right." Bud nodded. "We can't go pissing off the whites, you know. They can get pretty upset if they don't get the jobs that Hydro's promised them, eh. They might head to the Ledge and start protesting about their traditional rights or something. Two hundred years in this country must give them some kind of traditional rights, eh Sol?"

Sol's face was creased into a deep frown. "You guys shouldn't joke about shit like that," he said sharply.

"Relax, Sol, we're just having a bit of fun," Albert said.

"Fun is one thing," Sol said, "but we've worked way too hard on this goddamn dam thing with a shitload more work to come for people to make light of it. This is important work that we're doing for the Band and if you guys and the rest of the people in Grand Rapids don't appreciate all the work we do on your behalf, then what's the point in us doing it. What's the point of spending hours in meetings talking to fucking Hydro idiots and government morons? We do a lot of work for you guys and the rest of the community, but if you're always going to make fun of what we do, we might as well chuck it all in and let the white man take everything we got."

Bud started, "We were just joking that Albert probably has more Indian in him than you and me combined — " but Sol cut him off.

"Then Albert should get his fucking treaty number!" Sol shouted as he banged a fist on the steering wheel, sending a shudder throughout the truck. "If he doesn't have one, then he doesn't count as an Indian. You keep telling a guy that over and over again, but it just doesn't sink in. You never did care about a treaty number, did you Albert?"

"Treaty number makes no difference to me," Albert said bluntly. "Just a fucking waste of paper."

"See what I mean Bud? He doesn't know what's good for him."

Bud backed into his seat, saying nothing.

"You tell me what difference a treaty card would have made for me? It might have gotten you the job on this highway, but I still got one without one. And would I have caught more fish with it this winter with the extended season? Doubt it. How many fish did you catch with the extra two weeks you Indians got this winter? Eh Sol. How many?"

"Christ, Albert. That's not the point."

"Of course that's the point. Why should I want to spend two extra weeks on that fucking ice when I'm not going to get anything extra out it," said Albert. "That don't help me, so why should I have a treaty number anyway."

"You tell him Bud. How's your treaty number helping you?"

Bud raised his hands and held them in an appeasing motion in front of his face. "Hey don't get me in the middle of this. I'm just along for the ride."

"Yeah, leave Bud out of this, Sol. Even if he had a treaty number, he'd still get a job on the dam upgrade whenever they approve the goddamn thing."

"You think so? You think so?"

"I know so," Albert said.

"Well you're probably right there," Sol said. "But having a treaty number is more important than how many jobs we can get. It's important to the community because the more Indians we have who say they are Indians, the better it is for us. It's about respect, Albert. It's about saying to the white man that this is our community, these people with their cards are members of the community and should be respected. It's about accepting the fact that you're a fucking Indian."

"Don't need a card and a number to tell me that," Albert said. "You can tell just by looking at me that I'm an Indian. Makes no difference to any white man whether I have a card or a number."

"Sure it does, but then it also means that you have a whole community behind you and the white man better not fuck with you because if he does then he has to deal with everybody else in the Band," Sol said. "But that's not it Albert and you know it. The real reason you don't have a treaty number is if you don't have one, then you're not officially an Indian and if you're not officially an Indian, then you don't have to call yourself one. Like I said Albert, it's all about respect and the truth is that you've never respected the fact that you're an Indian. It's like you're ashamed of it."

Albert didn't respond; he just stared out of the window watching the trees and utility towers fly past. Bud stared at the road ahead, also staying quiet. Sol alternately watched the road ahead to keep the truck on track and looked out his side window at the trees. The only sound was the whine of the engine and the whistling of the wind through the open windows.

In the few minutes of uncomfortable silence, Albert finished off his beer and tossed the can out the window. It bounced once off the shoulder and flew into the ditch, landing with a small splash. Finally, he said, "Anyways, two years is a long time to wait for Hydro to figure out the dam upgrade. I might be retired by then."

Sol and Bud gave each other astonished looks and then laughed. "Retire!" Sol sputtered. "That I'd like to see."

"Yeah, I'd pay real good money to see that happen, you know," said Bud.

"I've been thinking 'bout retiring for a couple years now," Albert said indignantly. "Who knows, maybe next year's fishing season might be my last."

"Yeah right," Bud said.

"You can't afford to retire, Albert," said Sol. "Not only will you be broke but you'll go crazy home all day in your trailer."

"I'll find things to do."

"Like what. Hanging around Keung's driving Elaine crazy. It'll take only a week or two of that and she'll be filling out job application forms for you."

"Well, I have been thinking about it," Albert said quietly and then added, "retiring."

"Thinking about it is one thing," Sol said. "Doing it is something else."

The road north from Grand Rapids — Highway 6 — ended at a T-intersection at Ponton, a small village made up of a motel, a gas station, a small restaurant, a phone booth and some housing. The population of Ponton consisted of a single Korean family who owned and operated the motel, gas station and restaurant. The trio in the truck stopped for barely five minutes — enough for a fill-up and a quick bathroom break — before heading northeast on Highway 6, the main artery across the top of the province from Flin Flon towards Thompson and then on to York Factory. Unlike the shiny new blacktop they had been travelling, this section of the highway was a wreck. Deep ruts from all the traffic cut deeply into the pavement and the road heaved and undulated making vehicles rock back and forth like small boats on the lake during a high wind.

Sol now drove with two hands on the wheel. "Still think we should stop in Wabowden?" he asked.

"Wabowden?" Bud said with a slight whine. "What's in Wabowden?"

Sol ignored him. "What do you think Albert? Think we got time?"

Albert checked his watch. "Don't know. If the road's dry we'll be okay, if it's bad, it might slow us down."

"You're right. What time's the last ferry?"

"Eight o'clock, I think."

Bud cut in — "Please tell me we're not going to stop — "

Sol cut him off. "—That gives us four hours. That enough time?"

Albert shrugged. "Depends on the road. It rained last night back home but who knows if it rained up here. If it did, the road's going to be in bad shape."

"Yeah," Sol said with a sigh. "Better not chance it then, right?"

"Better not," Albert said with a shake of his head.

"Thank God. I'm glad we could all come to a decision here," Bud said sarcastically. "What's so important about stopping in Wabowden?"

Albert and Sol both chuckled. "The McQuire girls," Albert said.

"Steve and George," Sol added.

"Steve and George? What kind of girls are named Steve and George?" Bud demanded.

"The McQuire girls," Albert said quietly.

Sol said: "Actually they're real names aren't Steve and George" — "No shit," Bud said — "They're actually Stephanie and Georgiana but nobody ever calls them that."

"Except their old man, Jack McQuire, drunk son of a bitch that he was," Albert said.

"But since he's dead," Sol said, "everybody just calls them Steve and George."

"So what's the big deal about these McQuire girls?" Bud asked with a shrug. "Why make a special trip to Wabowden?"

Sol adjusted himself behind the wheel, twisting and cracking his shoulders and neck and then clearing the phlegm from this throat and spitting out the window. "Oh, after I finished high school there were no good jobs in Grand Rapids. This was just before Hydro started building the dam in Grand Rapids. They were doing a lot of studying at the time. Checking the land and annexing everything they could get their hands on, but it was still a few more years before they started to build the thing. The only place to get work was in Wabowden fixing up the railroad or working on the new road they were building up to Thompson."

"That's when I was running Jerry Harrison's old trapline in the winter and fishing on the lake in the summer and fall," Albert said. "After I quit working on Keweetan with Barings and Barry Fency."

"A job that I wanted to get, but then Abe stole it from me," Sol said.

"Sol was a couple years older," Albert said to Bud. "The captain didn't want to hire someone right out of high school. He wanted people with experience."

"That's bullshit!" Sol cried. "He hired you when you were seventeen."

"I told him I was older. I told him I was 21 and he told me he knew I was lying," Albert said. "But he thought I was pretending to be younger. He figured I was at least 25, especially when I told him I already had three years experience running a trapline and working on the railroad."

"So you also lied to him about the railroad?" Bud asked.

"No, I had three years on the railroad before the Keweetan. Unlike Sol I didn't finish high school. Grade Eight was as far as I got," Albert said. "Fourteen years old and my old lady kicks me out of the house and says 'Get to work, I can't support you no more.' So one of the few jobs that paid good enough and was willing to hire anyone was the railroad. That's why they hired Sol right out of high school."

"But who were these McQuire girls?" Bud asked.

"At the time when all this was happening, and even when I was on the Keweetan and Sol was still in school and after, during the years they were building the dam, the McQuire girls were special, famous throughout the area," Albert said. "Everyone from Thompson to Riverton had heard about the McQuire girls."

"People would travel for days to see them," Sol said. "Remember Billy Cunningham, Albert? He joined the army to go to Korea but the war ended before he got shipped out. So he decided to stay in the army and he did until he retired in 1980 in Vernon, in BC. But when he was in the army during those early years, before he got married, every time Billy Cunningham would get leave, a week here and a couple weeks there, he'd hop on a train or plane to Winnipeg, get on the Keweetan in Riverton and ride all the way up to Norman's Landing where Steve McQuire was waiting for him. He did this for probably five years until he got married."

"So what was so great about these girls?" Bud asked.

"What wasn't great about those girls," Sol said. "They were the best looking girls in the area. Steve was tall and lean like a movie star, not skinny like women in the movies today, but a healthy girl. When you danced with Steve, you knew you were dancing with a woman, not some fourteen year-old boy. She had these happy blue eyes and when she smiled at you, her whole face smiled. And when you told her a joke that was funny or said something she thought was funny, she laughed for real, out loud, like what you just said and the joke you told was the funniest thing in the world. She was a hell of a girl. George was shorter and a little bit heavier but everything was in the right places."

"Full-figured is what we used to call it," Albert jumped in. "Today, you young guys might think she was too fat, but she probably had the same figure as Marilyn Monroe, so that goes to show you."

Sol continued. "She had the bright blue eyes like her sister but she was more reserved, she wouldn't dance as much as Steve and if you said something remotely dirty, she'd blush and turn her head."

"So they were hookers then?" Bud said.

Albert laughed. "George and Steve weren't hookers."

Sol said: "If you wanted a hooker you went to Thompson or Winnipeg. George and Steve were girls from Wabowden."

Albert started in. "Abe once told me this story about this guy in the coffee shop in Wabowden. Steve was sitting by herself eating some soup and reading the paper and this guy sat down next to her, putting his arm around her. She brushed him off a couple of times and the guy got pissed off and started yelling at her. He called Steve a hooker, so she starts hitting this guy with her paper, yelling at him to get out. But then this guy who was having his lunch on a day off, Abe says, goes over and grabs the other guy by the hair, drags him out of the coffee shop and kicks his fucking ass out of town."

Sol chuckled. "That wasn't just any guy having lunch on his day off."

"What the hell you talking about?" Albert said. "I'm the one who heard the story. Not you."

Sol chuckled again. "I just said that wasn't just any guy having lunch."

"No shit," Albert said. "That was the guy that kicked the shit out of another guy who called Steve McQuire a hooker."

"That was Abe," Sol said plainly.

"Who was Abe?" Bud asked. "The guy who called her a hooker?"

"Abe wouldn't call anyone a hooker," Albert said.

"No, Abe was the other guy," Sol said.

There was a second of stunned silence before Albert shouted. "That was Abe?" He whirled to face the other side of the truck. His quick motion knocked Bud into Sol and the truck jerked into the other lane. Sol yanked the truck back quickly, caught the edge of the road and the truck leaned towards the ditch. A cloud of dust blew out from the back.

Bud grabbed with both hands for the dashboard. "Watch the fuckin' road!" he shouted.

Sol fought back onto the road and the truck shimmied and bounced several times on the uneven pavement before straightening. Once Sol got everything under control, he slugged Bud on the shoulder. "Jesus Christ, Bud. What the fuck were you doing?"

"Hey, don't look at me. It was Albert freaking out over here."

"That couldn't have been Abe!" Albert said, oblivious to all the excitement. "Abe always said someone else dragged the guy out of the coffee shop. Abe wouldn't do something like that."

Sol muttered under his breath but continued with the story Albert had started. "The jerk who called Steve a hooker was some idiot from Ontario who was working on the railroad with us. When Abe heard what he said, he dragged him out of the coffee shop and kicked the shit out of him around the corner. And then he went back to see if Steve was okay. She was and she was also extremely appreciative of what Abe did, standing up for her honour and all that."

Albert looked out the window. "I can't believe Abe lied to me all these years about that. I just can't believe it."

Sol continued: "And when the jerk regained consciousness, he made an even bigger mistake and went to the local RCMP constable to report how Abe beat the shit out of him. When old Dan asked the guy why someone like Abe would beat the shit out of him, the guy made his final mistake and told Dan why. He told him he called Steve a hooker. Well Dan Lukacinsky grabbed the guy, handcuffed him and threw him in jail for three days, the time it took till the Keweetan pulled into Norman's Landing. Dan escorted him to the boat and told him never to show his face around Norway House again because everybody would know that he called Steve McQuire a hooker and they'd be lining up to take turns beating the crap of him."

Albert shook his head. "I just can't believe Abe lied to me about that."

"Abe's probably told you plenty of lies," Sol said with a shrug. "Get used to it."

"But Steve never mentioned knowing your brother. Didn't think Abe was the type. Just goes to show you."

"You know that Steve never talked about who she knew," said Sol. "That's why she and her sister were so popular. When you went out with them, they would never talk about who they saw last night or the week before, even though you were probably best friends with the guy."

"So if these girls weren't hookers, what were they?" Bud asked.

Albert sighed and looked at the muskeg rush by the truck. Several seconds passed before he answered. "If you wanted a hooker at the time of the McQuire girls, you could go to Thompson on your days off or talk to Maggie Kellock at the tavern in Norway House. But if you wanted something else, something nice, something where you didn't feel like a piece of shit afterward and something where everybody didn't look at you funny, then you went out with Steve or George."

"You had to ask them out too, about a week in advance," Sol added. "You couldn't just show up and expect them to go out with you, even if they were sitting at home alone. And it wasn't because there were a lot of guys wanting to take them out. Well, there were, but even so, they expected you to ask them out in advance, just like you would any other girl. And you had to take them on a date, dancing, to a movie when there was one in town, or for some coffee and some pastry at the coffee shop."

Albert took over. "And you had to take a bath before the date and dress as best as you could. Some of the guys didn't have any real good clothes so they had to borrow from their co-workers or friends so they could take out one of the McQuire girls. And you had to treat them right, too."

"You had to bring flowers or candy and do things like open doors for them, pulling chairs so they could sit or hold out your arm for them when you went walking," said Sol.

"You had to act like a gentleman," Albert added.

"Right," said Sol. "Like a gentleman."

Sol and Albert went silent so Bud spoke up. "So why did everybody get excited about these girls. If you had to act like gentlemen and get all prettied up just to go on a date with these girls, why did everybody waste their time?"

Sol filled him in. "Because the McQuire girls treated you special. You knew they dated everybody else in town, but when you took out Steve or George, you felt like you were their boyfriend. They were interested in your work or what you did, even though it took most guys about an hour to get over the discomfort of being on a date with a real woman. They laughed at your jokes if they were funny, and if they weren't funny, they'd give you a look that said it wasn't funny, but didn't make you feel stupid. They wanted to know how your day was or where you were from or how your mom was doing. They talked about politics and current events and you started going to the library to read up on things so the next time you went out with them, you'd be able to talk with them about what the Prime Minister meant when he said something. They made you feel like you were important, like you were something special, and weren't just some stupid kid working on the railroad. You mattered because Steve and George made you feel like you mattered."

"But then they probably let you fuck them," Bud said pointing his finger. "That's why all you guys went out with them."

Albert shook his head. "It was more than that. Just because you had a date with them didn't mean they'd give you an easy fuck. You'd have to earn it over time."

"First they'd teach you how to kiss right," Sol said. "Most of us thought you'd just shove your tongue down a woman's throat, but the McQuire girls would go through the process step by step like they were teaching you how to build a box or fix an engine. And once they figured you knew what you were doing, they'd let you touch them so you'd know how to touch a woman. Same way as kissing, they'd work with you step by step, slowing you down because you'd be all excited and be grabbing and pulling and clutching. Everything was slow down, take your time, don't get it all over in a couple of seconds because it's no fun that way. Some guys couldn't take it and they'd want to move faster, but Steve and George wouldn't let them. If they complained or wouldn't learn anything, then there'd be no more dates. Those guys would then always head north to Thompson or talk to

Maggie Kellock. Most of the time you'd just see them drinking in the tavern."

"So if you passed all that shit, they'd give you a final exam?" Bud asked with a laugh.

"Pretty much," Albert said. "But they'd work you in slowly, make you remember to take your time, treat them right and have fun. Once you graduated, you pretty much knew what you were doing, and since you knew what made them feel good, they were glad to see ya. You still had to dress up, have a bath and take them somewhere nice, but you both knew that it was going to get pretty hot for both of you that night."

"That's why Billy Cunningham was always welcome back home during his leave," Sol said. "They taught him right and they knew that he knew what he was doing."

Bud grabbed the dashboard and started bouncing in his seat, like a dog in the cab of a truck. "So are we going to Wabowden to meet the McQuire girls?"

Albert and Sol laughed. "Jesus, Bud. Put it back in your pants. Stevie and George are probably almost 70 years old. Still lookers at their age but past their prime for someone like you."

Bud deflated and fell back into the seat. "Fuck! Guess I'm stuck with you old guys."

Albert shrugged. "There's always Maggie Kellock."

"She still alive?" Sol asked.

"Yep. And I guess for Bud's sake we could always stop by the nursing home and see if she could help him out, for old time's sake."

"Aww man. You guys are sick," Bud said. "I don't know why I came on this trip with you guys, anyways."

Sol shrugged, and with an arm hanging out the window and one hand on the steering wheel kept the truck as steady as he could on the undulating road. "What the hell else you going to do. Nothing happening in Grand Rapids. Right now, all the action's in Norway House."

2

Conversation between the three was pretty much impossible once Sol made the turn off Hwy. 6 onto the road to Norway House. Hwy. 45 to Norway House was a long, flat sheet of heavy white gravel. Unlike the main highways in the province, those stolid orderly roads which seemed to be sliced smoothly through the forest with surgical skill, Hwy. 45 was gouged into the landscape, a jagged, angry wound, recently healed, scar tissue barely formed. Uncivilized weeds, grass and brush grew right up to the edge of the road, forming a waist-high border of vegetation that staggered and wavered whenever a vehicle drove past. The treeline on both sides of the road was ragged and threadbare. Trees that still remained at the edge and had once threatened to usurp the road were savagely pruned back. Sol's truck shuddered and swayed, and rocks and pebbles battered and buffeted the undercarriage, creating a symphony of percussion and vibration that drowned out any chance for words. A layer of grit built in the cab, and every time another vehicle passed in the opposite direction it trailed a cloud of dust that dropped the visibility around the truck and sent Bud into a brief hacking fit.

After a fourth vehicle passed them going the other way, Sol slowed the truck to about half the speed and leaned against the door to reach into his pocket. He pulled out a pack of smokes, flipped it open and tossed it onto the dash in front of him. Several cigarettes tumbled out and he grabbed one, putting it into his mouth. He then reached over, pushed in the truck cigarette lighter and waited. Bud gave him a perplexed look.

"You want one?" Sol shouted to be heard above the turbulence, pointing at the scattering of cigarettes on the dash. "Go ahead." Bud shook his head, but watched intently as Sol grabbed the popped lighter and held the glowing red circle to light his smoke. Sol took a long deep puff and then blew the smoke to the roof. It furled and floated throughout the cab. Bud coughed several times. Sol replaced the lighter, gripped the wheel with both hands and sped up again. The cigarette remained in his mouth and he shook his lower lip to flick the burnt ashes off of the cigarette. Bud continued to look at him, and after several seconds Sol gestured with his chin towards the dash. "If you want one go ahead," he shouted out of the side of his mouth.

Bud shook his head. "Why are you smoking?"

"Get's rid of the dust," Sol shouted back.

"You're kidding."

Sol shook his head. "The smoke creates a buffer which keeps the dust from accumulating."

"You're kidding, right?"

Sol shook his head. Bud turned to Albert. He was blinking profusely and breathing heavily through his nose. "He's kidding, right?" Albert shrugged but said nothing. Bud turned back to face the front and was hit by a hack attack, his coughing coming deep from his throat and doubling him over in the seat. When it ended, he sat up, his face hot and flushed and tears streaming down his face. "I think it's making it worse." His voice cracked and crumbled and he was hit again by another attack.

Sol continued his cigarette and Albert stared out the window. When the second attack finished, Bud turned to Albert. "I think he's making it worse!" Albert shrugged again and said nothing.

Bud turned back to Sol. "I think your smoking's making it worse. I can hardly breathe." He coughed again.

Sol sucked one last long puff from the cigarette and then spat it towards the floor near his door. It bounced once off the edge of the seat and fell to the carpet. Sol quickly stamped it out with his free foot. He dropped the speed of the truck again, grabbed another cigarette and pressed in the lighter.

"You're not having another are you?" Bud asked. "What are you trying to do, kill me?"

"It'll help kill the dust," Sol insisted.

"Bullshit. It only makes things worse. If it's going to kill something, it'll kill me."

"Okay, but it helps me relax while I drive this goddamn road. Every fucking year they keep saying they'll be paving it, but every year it's the same goddamn thing." The lighter popped and Sol lit his cigarette. "Smoking makes sure I stay calm so we don't fucking lose control on this gravel and crash into the trees." Bud began hacking again as Sol accelerated the truck. Sol briefly laid his hand on Bud's back. "Sorry about this, Bud. Hopefully you get used to it by the time we reach Norway House."

In between his hacks, Bud muttered incoherently. "What'd you say?" Sol asked.

It took several more seconds of hacking before Bud had enough strength to repeat himself. "I said we should have taken a boat instead," he said, before launching into another series of devastating coughs.

Sol finally got the truck up to speed and flicked another set of ashes with a shake of his lower lip. A vehicle sped by in the other direction and the truck was enveloped in another dark cloud of dust. Sol puffed deeply on the cigarette. When he let the smoke out, he inhaled it again through his nose. "Think you're right there, Bud, but Albert didn't feel like taking the boat!"

"Why not?"

"You'd have to ask Albert 'bout that."

Bud turned to Albert, but Albert said nothing. "Why didn't we take the boat Albert?" Bud asked. Albert's answer was a shrug so Bud started to ask again. Suddenly his eyes went wide with realization and he quickly gestured with his index finger. "Ohhh, I get it, you — " he started to say, but his words got caught in a coughing fit.

The landscape remained unchanged for another 90 minutes until they came over a rise and everything changed so suddenly that Sol lifted his foot off the gas pedal and the truck slowly drifted to a stop. The three men stared wide-eyed at the scene of devastation and regeneration. It seemed to stretch endlessly on both sides of the road. Anything taller than three feet was dead. What used to be a universe of thriving green trees was now a collection of exhausted stalks of brown and black kindling, thousands of skeletal figures frozen in rigor mortis, like crucified corpses stripped of all life and left to rot. The floor of the forest, however, was teeming with new life, small trees, shrubs and grasses, all the same shade of light green, new green, with the colour of sun still mixed in. They were the offspring of seeds long dormant, finally given their chance to propagate and grow, feasting on the corpse of the forest, their dead ancestor, in a mad dash to rise above it all and become the new rulers, the new forest.

"Jesus Christ," Sol said with a whistle.

"Didn't think it'd be so bad, but there it is," Albert said.

"Man, I never seen it so bad," Bud said. "Must have been some fire."

"One of the biggest, that's what Leo said. Ripped through here like a bandit," Albert said.

"Amazing thing he survived," said Sol.

"Who survived?" asked Bud.

"Fency's boy," Sol replied. "He was in this."

Bud nodded his head. "Oh yeaaaah. I heard something about that. What the hell happened to him?"

"Nobody really knows. They just found a couple of them drifting a few hundreds yards off the lake near Norman's Landing. Both burned pretty bad and some pretty nasty smoke inhalation. Fency's boy spent, what was it Albert, six weeks?"

"Probably eight, I think," Albert said.

"Something like that."

"Jesus," said Bud, and after a pause he asked: "Anybody ever ask him what happened?"

Albert and Sol shrugged. The trio stared at the regenerating forest for a few more minutes and then climbed back into the truck. By the time they reached the ferry, Bud's coughing fits were getting shorter and shorter. The road became paved the last 100 yards before the river so Sol extinguished his smoke in the ashtray. He rolled down his window and a blast of fresh clean air blew in, dispersing the dust and the smoke. Bud sucked deeply at the air, gasping like a dying fish.

Sol laughed and slapped Bud on the shoulder. "That wasn't so bad was it Bud?"

"Fuck that," Bud said. "A few times back there, I wasn't sure if I was going to make it."

"But you did. So here we are."

Sol pulled his truck right up to the lip of the dock. The flatbed ferry sat on the opposite shore of the Nelson, loading a few vehicles. The three men got out of the truck and stretched. Bud walked up to the river, bent down to his knees and splashed water on his face and neck. When he finished cleaning, he stood up, unzipped and pissed in the same spot.

Albert and Sol looked at each other. Sol raised his eyebrows. "Bet you a lot of people do that," Sol shouted out to Bud.

"What's that?" Bud said over his shoulder.

"Never mind. Here comes the ferry."

Bud quickly finished his business, zipped up and ran back to the truck. "Okay if I drive 'er on?" he asked as he climbed into the driver's seat.

"Knock yourself out," Sol said with a shrug. "Keys are in it."

"All right!" Bud said, and he jumped behind the wheel. He started up the truck and leaned on the steering wheel, his face all lit up like a kid at Christmas, waiting for the ferry to come.

The ferry was a long, metal flatbed the width of two tractor trailers and the length of one. Blue steel fencing ran along the sides, and at each end was an extended sheet of metal plating that rose to about 35 degrees when the ferry was out in the water and then dropped flat and acted as a ramp to the shore. It crossed by using a winch that pulled it along the length of a two-inch cable stretched across the width of the Nelson River. An operator controlled the winch from a small booth at the southwest corner of the ferry. When the ferry pulled up to the north side of the river, the ramp came down and the three trucks pulled away. Albert and Sol climbed aboard, waving to the operator. The operator waved back, and once Bud gingerly steered the truck onto the ferry, it started its journey back to the south side. Albert and Sol walked up to the operator booth. The operator held a joystick in one hand and waved again with his other. He was of average height with a bit of a paunch showing from underneath his black and white flannel shirt. His jeans were faded and dirty and his brown boots were mud-crusted, the laces tied only halfway up, leaving the top few holes empty. His face had strong, native features, thin slits for eyes, a short flat nose with full lips. Combined with his salt and pepper goatee and a red ballcap that he wore backwards, he looked more Asian than Native. And like Albert and Sol, his face was wrinkled and weather-beaten, but he was much younger. He pursed his lips in greeting. "Hey Albert. Hey Sol. How's it going?"

"Hey Joel," Albert said, sticking out his hand. Joel looked at the hand, as if wondering what to do with it, but then reciprocated.

"Hey Joel," Sol said, also shaking hands with the man. "Been busy."

"More than usual. York Boat days you know. That's why you guys have come?"

Sol nodded. "Yep."

"You too Albert?"

Albert nodded. "I'm looking to visit Leo and Bernie."

There was a quick look of fear on Joel's face and then it disappeared. He nodded sympathetically. "Oh yeah, Bernie. How she doing?"

"Not too good," Albert said with a shrug. "Some days not bad, some days worse. More worse days than good though, so . . . you know."

"Yeah, that cancer can be pretty bad I hear. Say hi and sorry when you see Leo, okay?"

"Yeah I'll tell him you said that."

"Sorry to hear about Barry Fency. Knew his boy a bit, we were a couple years apart in school," Joel said. "Is it true what they said about him?"

"Are they saying things about Fency's boy?" Albert asked.

"No. 'Bout his old man. Said he disappeared or something before he died?"

"Wouldn't know anything about that," Albert said with a huff. "Sounds like a bunch of crap talk to me."

"Well, that's what they're saying."

Sol stepped up quickly and leaned into the booth to look at the controls. "So how's the old man, Joel? Still trapping is he?"

Joel laughed. "He thinks he is. He set his trapline this year but with the forest fire and all, he barely got anything at all. But he was out there every day, checking his lines, expecting something."

"Never gives up does he?"

"Nope, told him he should retire, give up the trapline, maybe let some kid handle it, but he won't listen. Almost broke his hip last summer but he was out there in November setting his lines and looking for animals."

"Fuckin' old bugger," Sol said with a smile. "He'll probably die out there."

"Wouldn't surprise me," Joel said.

"He going to be in the York Boat Races?"

"Doctor won't let him. Doesn't mind him doing his trapline but he draws the line at him in a York Boat. Told him he had a choice: go into the York Boat races, and wreck his hip so bad he can't set his line, or forget the races and keep walking."

The ferry pulled up to the other side and the ramp began to lower. Bud revved up the truck, so Albert and Sol headed towards it. "Of course that didn't stop the old bugger from signing up as a caller for a team," Joel shouted at them. "If he can't row at least he can be out there."

"Son of a bitch. Tell him Sol says hey."

"I'll do that," Joel said. "And say hi to Leo and Bernie for me when you see them, will you Albert?"

Albert followed Sol into the truck and waved back. "Will do."

As soon as the ramp hit the ground, Bud slipped the truck into gear and roared away for the last few miles to Norway House.

The town of Norway House was actually a collection of villages and housing developments stretched across several islands and peninsulas formed as Lake Winnipeg drained into the Nelson River. The river took the water and carried on northeast until it emptied into Hudson Bay between Port Nelson and York Factory. The first settlers of Norway House were originally intent on traveling further into Western Canada but when Jake McLeod broke his arm in late Fall, the group of settlers, made up of Sinclairs, Apetagons, McLeods and other families from the Shetland Islands, decided to stop for the winter while Jake McLeod's arm healed. By the time spring came, they had established a strong enough foundation for a town and developed so deep a relation-ship with the local natives that they decided to stay. A few members of the party continued, only to be stopped by the grand rapids of the Saskatchewan River, but the majority of the party settled in, consorted with the natives and built a home that they later called Norway House. The village's strategic and shielded location up the Nelson, north of the lake, protected it from most onslaughts of weather that the lake threw to the north shore. Although it was cold in the winter and hot and gorged with mosquitoes and black flies in the summer, Norway House was the perfect location as a distribution centre for the developing northwest. Supplies, people, fur, trade goods and anything else traveling through northwest Canada was channeled through Norway House. The village grew into a town, and soon the fur trading companies decided that building York boats in Norway House by using the abundant trees made more sense than shipping them from York Factory. For decades, Norway House was a hub of activity, and then several hundred miles to the south the Trans-Continental railroad was built, and soon York boats were no longer needed to carry goods and people to the west. Activity dropped, people left and even with the hydro activity in the mid 20th century, Norway House was isolated from most of the country. Its only link to the outside world was the Keweetan and its two barges. Even that link didn't really connect with Norway House. Because of its size, the Keweetan was unable to travel up the Nelson to Norway House, so goods had to be carried by smaller boats or horse power up the trail from Norman's Landing. The government finally built a road to Norway House in the late 70s, but decided it wasn't worth paving.

Bud pulled the truck off the road into the parking lot of the new Norway House Recreation Centre. The building was long and wide, full of clean clear glass with a massive circular carving of a fish bursting with freedom from the surface of an inviting lake. The image was surrounded by the words Kinnseaw-sipi, the First Nation Community of Norway House. The three men stared, mouths agape, at the new building.

"Man's that something," Bud said.

"Sure went up fast," Sol said. "When were we here last? Two, three years ago Albert?"

"Two, I think. No more than three."

"Pretty fast, then. The new chief seems to be doing good."

"Dick Sinclair's boy isn't it?" Bud asked.

"Yep, Johnny or Jackie or something or the other. He's a young go-getter right out of law school."

"Nothing like the old man, eh Albert?" Sol said.

"No shit."

"Lazy is he?" Bud asked.

"Dick Sinclair," Albert said with a huff. "Probably the laziest bastard in Norway House. Can't stop drinking enough to last three weeks on one job so he lives off his treaty cheque in his treaty house."

"Wonder where his boy got all his initiative?" Bud asked.

"Who knows. Maybe laziness skips a generation," Sol said. "Been known to happen." He turned to Albert. "So what's the story Albert. You want us to come to Leo's or should we just hang out here."

Albert shook his head. "I think it's better if I go by myself. I don't how Bernie's doing so it's probably no good that the three of us show up all at once. You don't mind me taking the truck?"

"What's yours is mine," Sol said. "Bud and I will hang out here and check out the newfangled cultural centre, right Bud?"

Bud shrugged. "Whatever. I'm just a passenger on this trip."

Sol and Bud headed towards the cultural centre. Albert jumped into the truck and headed off to visit his brother.

3

Albert's brother Leo lived in the southeast part of Norway House, across the bridge from the reserve and a couple of kilometres south of the old cemetery. His was a grey Indian Affairs designed three-bedroom bungalow that sat on a hill just above the banks of the Nelson River. It had no basement and stood like a mobile home, set up on planks of wood, and Albert figured it probably shook like heck in heavy breezes. It was similar to most of the homes in the area, all of them built without basements for two reasons: at the time of their construction, Indian Affairs didn't want to pay for the extra costs of digging out the ground and laying down foundations; and, because of the town's proximity to the river and possible flooding, it was considered less trouble not to have a basement to flood.

Albert parked in the gravel driveway behind his brother's pickup and climbed out. He turned slowly to stare at the scenery around him. It was an eerie sight: the forest from the bridge up to the point was dense, the trees lush with leaves and the ground cover so thick with brush it was almost impenetrable. But just to the west of Leo's house it was a totally different world. There were no trees, only thin black stalks of burnt wood and the bright green of new brush starting to thicken but nowhere near the old forest behind him. The definition between the old and the dead stretched north and south, curving slightly on the opposite side of the river and disappearing in the distance. About ten meters from Leo's house was a pile of burnt rubble.

"Heck of a scene," a voice said behind him. "Fire was so big it jumped the river and just roared on by, barely missing the house. Like someone ran a torch along that side and left this side alone."

Albert gave his brother Leo a quick glance. "It's incredible. That Fency's house over there?"

"What's left of it. Amazing the boy made it through alive. Tough to lose his house like that, but it's the best thing that ever happened to him."

"He was lucky there."

"The Lord was looking out, at least for him," Leo said, looking up to the sky and giving a quick cross. Like Albert, Leo was tall and board shouldered, with a heavy stomach that hung over his belt a little lower than Albert's and caused the space between his shirt buttons to stretch out. Although their facial characteristics were similar, Leo's skin tone was darker and his features leaned more closely to the native side of the family. There were wrinkles around his eyes, but since he was younger they were not as pronounced as Albert's. Out of all of his brothers and sisters, Albert liked Leo the best because he never seemed to blame anyone for his problems and also seemed to have a permanent smirk on his face, as if he were constantly thinking about a joke he had heard the other day, or knew something about you that you thought you'd kept secret.

"I hear Fency's boy is doing well in Grand Rapids," Leo said.

Albert nodded. "He's fishing with his old man's boat and license."

"I heard about that. Sorry about Barry."

"Yeah," was all he said.

Leo placed his hand on Albert's shoulder and squeezed. "It's good to see you Albert. I'm really glad you came up."

"Not every day your little brother becomes a minister. Elaine says she's sorry she couldn't make it, but you know how things are at Keung's during the summer. She's' got so many American fishermen stopping in that there's no free time."

Leo smiled and nodded. "I knew she'd come if she could. Give her a big kiss when you see her again."

"I will," Albert said, and then the two brothers went silent and stared at the forest fire remnants for several more seconds. Finally, Leo slapped Albert on the shoulder and broke the silence. "Hey let's not stand out here all day, Albert," he said, steering them towards the house. "Come on inside and say hi to Bernie."

Albert followed Leo into the house. There was a slight entrance that ran past a kitchen that was so tiny there was barely enough space for one person of Albert's size. With his brother outweighing him by about 40 pounds, Albert wondered how Leo managed to cook meals in the puny space. There was barely any counter space, maybe a couple of feet on each side of the sink with every single inch of that space covered with dirty plates and pots. The fridge and the stove were both half-size models, but in the small kitchen space they appeared to be massive appliances. A lingering scent of fish that was probably several days old hung in the air. The dimness of the light from a tiny window over the sink made the room look dirtier than it actually was. The place wasn't filthy and disgusting — the floor looked recently mopped and there wasn't any garbage thrown around the room — it was just a little messy. It had probably been only a couple days since someone tidied up the place.

Leo led Albert past the small kitchen and into the living room. It was a few times larger than the kitchen, but a whole lot brighter. A huge picture window, framed by bright, apple-green curtains, almost covered the entire wall, giving a complete view of the slope leading to the river and the lush island, that at this point in the river, split it in two tributaries. Directly outside the glass hung several bird feeders that were visited every few seconds by various species of small, colourful birds. Elaine would know what kind of birds they were, but to Albert they were just little birds. They would dart in, perch on the ledges of the feeders, grab a few seeds and then dart out again. Once in awhile a bird would stop for a second, chirp a quick song and then grab some seeds and fly off. Someone had taped a few strips of masking tape onto the glass so that birds would not mistake the huge window for an empty space. Wind chimes dangled near the feeders, offering a brief percussive harmony to the songs of the birds. A large bumblebee, thick as Albert's thumb, bounced off the pane of glass several times, searching for a way through the invisible barrier. It traveled halfway across the glass and then decided enough was enough and flew off. There were plenty of blossoms, wildflowers, and dandelions scattered along the slope and the bee headed in that direction.

The room was made even brighter by a large mirror that hung on the right wall perpendicular to the window. It reflected the entire room, making it seem twice the size. The mirror also offered vistas that couldn't be seen by directly looking out the window. Albert could see other parts of Leo's yard; his small boat drifting in the lake and tied to a tree stump; the leftover wreckage of the Fency trailer home, a skeleton of black beams; the wind on the river at the end of the island; and to the south, the bright green of recovering woods juxtaposed with the dead stalks of burnt trees.

Below the mirror was a full-sized hospital bed. A couple of monitors were situated just off the head and they hummed quietly, keeping track of whatever they were supposed to keep track of. A series of IV drips hung from a hook like a mobile, their transparent lines stringing down from their bags towards the bed and into Bernie's arm. The mattress was completely surrounded by pillows, blankets and a variety of plush soft toys, all designed to prevent Bernie from striking any hard surfaces with her body. Leo's wife was suffering from bone cancer, and the disease had slowly destroyed her bones so much that in the past couple of years she had suffered several minor fractures just by accidentally banging an arm, a hand, a foot, against the side of the bed or the wall.

After looking about the room and the river and birds outside the window, Albert finally decided to look at Bernie. She was much smaller than he remembered, but then that could be the bed and all the pillows. She had been living with bone cancer for a couple of years now, and even though she had lost almost a hundred pounds since Albert had last seen her a year ago, she looked peaceful, like a sleeping child unconcerned and unaware of bad things in the world. She seemed tranquil and calm, and her face, although pale and gaunt, did not show the lifeless pallor that Albert had seen in other cancer victims. Barry Fency didn't look like this, in his last moments.

It could have been the light from the outside, but it was probably something deeper. Bernie had always been a strong woman. She had to have been to stick with his brother through his drinking, his temper and the loss of their son Eddie.

Eddie had disappeared six years ago, taking a bag full of clothes and driving Leo's boat all the way to Grand Rapids. From there, he probably hitched a ride with a trucker or a hunter down to Winnipeg. After that, nobody really knew. The police didn't bother to look because since Eddie was just over sixteen, he was considered more of a runaway than a missing kid. Bernie and Leo had heard nothing from Eddie since then. There were rumours, but nothing definite.

The event changed Leo's life, surprisingly for the better. Leo and Bernie, one of the hardest drinking and fighting couples in Norway House, turned themselves completely around. They managed to give up the booze, first Leo, and then Bernie, and then to look for some peace in their lives. Bernie found it in foster children, kids like her lost son Eddie, needing a place to stay. In the years between Eddie's disappearance and Bernie's diagnosis of cancer, more than twenty kids had called this tiny bungalow home, at least for a little while. Leo had loved the children and tried to help in the way he couldn't help his son, but his peace was located somewhere else. He headed back to the Anglican Church, dropping in on the odd Sunday, and then it was once a week. Since he was good with his hands, he volunteered as the caretaker and handyman for the little Anglican Church in Rossdale, fixing up minor electrical and plumbing problems. Slowly he became more involved, talking with the minister and the bishops as they came through town. After a couple of years, they needed a deacon because John Roberts had retired, moving to a nursing home near Winnipeg to be closer to his grandkids. Leo seemed the logical choice. And after four years, because the little Anglican Church in Rossdale needed a minister when Rev. Benson move to Calgary by invitation of the new archbishop there, Leo was asked if he wanted to be ordained as a minister of the church. He said yes, partly because he figured he was going to need something to do with himself once Bernie passed on.

As Albert looked at Bernie, he could see that she wasn't ready to give up. There was a lot of strength in her fragile body, and even as she slept, surrounded by the hospital equipment and her gauntlet of protective pillows, her face still shone with the glow of life.

Albert watched her for a few seconds, allowed a bit of Bernie's peace to rub off, and then backed off. Although there was joy in watching her sleep, he didn't want to become an intruder into Bernie's calm world of light and birds. Albert glanced at his brother. Leo was looking at his wife, smiling slightly. For those brief seconds, he seemed to have forgotten that Albert was in the same room. Leo leaned forward to brush the hair that had fallen into Bernie's face, but stopped his hand a foot above her. His fingers waggled, as if he were trying to move the hair without touching her. He did this for several seconds, turned his hand into a fist and brought it up to his mouth.

Albert felt the discomfort of intruding more deeply, so he stepped away and looked towards the kitchen. "Think I should go," he whispered, but Leo turned and reached the hand out to him. Leo's eyes glistened as he stepped up and placed that hand on Albert's shoulder, holding him in place.

"Stay," he said quietly, almost whispering the word. "Bernie won't like it if she heard you were here and she missed you. She'll wake up from her nap soon." He gave Albert's shoulder a quick squeeze and then gestured for Albert to follow him down the hallway that branched perpendicularly from the kitchen doorway. "Let's go to my room. I've still got some things to get ready for tonight so come on, we'll go there for a bit. It's been awhile since I've seen you, Albert, and I'm not going to let you leave so fast."

Albert nodded and before he followed his brother, he gave one last look at Bernie and her world.

4

Leo's room was the last one of three, at the end of the hall, on the same side of the house as the kitchen. Because it was on the north side and the window was completely covered by Venetian blind, it was so much darker than the bright living room that Albert had difficulty seeing. The room was small, just a little bit larger than the kitchen but not by much. It was also very bare. There were only two pieces of furniture in the room: a twin bed, impossibly small for his larger brother, and a small wooden end table. The bed was covered by a harsh wool blanket with the image of Jesus Christ's face covering its entire surface. The end table had only enough room for a Bible, a half full glass of water and a square black clock radio, the time blinking in red LED light. On the wall over the head of the bed hung a painting of Jesus Christ crucified on the cross, the glow of the heavens emanating from his tortured, yet peaceful body, and the hands of mourning disciples reaching up in sorrow and anguish as clouds parted above, angels speeding down to carry Jesus home.

On the wall nearest the door was a smaller photo, a simple 3X5 stuck to the wall by a couple of coloured tacks. Albert leaned closer to get a better look of the photo. It was Leo's family, taken just outside this same house in somewhat happier times. Leo was a few pounds lighter and without the streaks of grey he now had. Bernie was without disease, her large and full body laughing at something that had happened just prior to the photo being taken, and Eddie, their son, even at that young age, standing taller than both of his parents, his serious adolescent face trying to remain stoic, but with the beginnings of a grin creeping over his face as he watched his mother laughing. Albert felt the affection and tenderness of the photo, probably more than seven years old, its warmth the only cheer in the room.

Albert felt chilled in his brother's room. It was a cell, bare and cold, like the cabin in which he had found Jerry Harrison's body so many years back, the walls trying to squeeze all the life out of the place. Leo moved to shut the door behind him but Albert said, "If it's all right, could you keep that open? It's kind of stuffy and

I've been riding in Sol's truck for the past five hours." It was a bit of a lie but Albert needed some reason to prevent Leo from closing him into this room.

"Sure thing," Leo said, leaving the door open. Some light from the bright living room managed to make its way down the hallway and Albert felt a little less chilled. Not much, but enough to keep him from thinking disturbing thoughts about finding Jerry Harrison's dead body in his rundown cabin. Leo gestured to the bed. "Have a seat."

Albert looked at the benevolent image of Jesus' face staring up from the blanket and moved to the end of the bed, perching on the edge so he didn't have to sit his entire butt on the Savior's face.

Leo sat down next to Albert, directly on the Lord's nose. He placed a hand on his brother's shoulder. He spoke in a hushed voice, one normally saved for church or a funeral. "I'm truly sorry about Barry. I knew he was a good friend of yours. It's hard when something like that happens. You know what's going to happen and think you're prepared for it but when it does, it still shocks the hell out of you. Of course, everybody's talking about all the craziness that happened. The damnedest thing him disappearing like that." Leo leaned closer and whispered as if they were sharing secrets. "Did they ever find him? Or his body?"

Albert fidgeted. He was uncomfortable sitting on the edge of the bed, and worked hard to keep from sliding to the floor, but he was unwilling to sit on Leo's blanket. The tone of Leo's conversation also wasn't helping things. He barely managed to shake his head in response to his brother's questions.

"Do you think that he actually managed to walk out of the hospital on his own? Did he have that much strength? It's amazing when you hear of something like that. It's almost biblical, don't you think? A man on his deathbed disappearing into the night. I know the story is that he died and they must have lost his body, but how can something like that happen? How can a hospital lose the body of a dead man? It's too incredible to believe."

Albert tried not to listen to his brother and fought to stay on the bed without looking as if he were fighting to stay on the bed. He focused his gaze on the photo of Leo's family. Somebody, probably the photographer, must have said something funny to make Bernie laugh out loud like that. And it must have been extremely funny to break Eddie's tough facade. Albert wondered if it was a joke or whether someone was poking fun at Leo. His face seemed somewhat annoyed and Albert knew that Eddie would have found anybody making fun of his old man pretty hilarious. But he wouldn't have laughed at Leo, because at that time in their lives, Leo was not a man to be trifled with. He was an ugly, angry man in those years, full of beer and quick to strike. Which is why Eddie packed up and left without telling anyone where he was going.

Leo still must have been talking about the disappearance of Barry's body because his face was stunned when Albert jerked his chin towards the photo and asked, "Ever hear anything 'bout Eddie?"

Leo's face lost all of its colour, and in his surprised face, vestiges of that old temper flared up for a brief second. Albert wasn't afraid of Leo — his temper was nothing compared to that of their mother — but he needed some reason to stop Leo's continuous questions and monologue about the disappearance of Barry Fency's body. Leo quickly got his temper under control. He looked at the photo, his face drifting away, as he searched for the memory of the day and the thoughts of his lost son.

"Might be in the army somewhere," he whispered. "Jack Dawson heard from his brother-in-law's cousin or something like that, that someone in the army, that someone with Eddie's name was stationed in Cyprus. Peacekeeping and all that. Guess he learned all about that growing up in this house."

Albert nodded, finally deciding to forget Jesus and sit completely on the bed. "He's doing all right. Eddie was always a smart, tough kid. He knew how to take care of himself."

"Yeah," Leo said, "he did. That's why he left."

"He's all right. I know that. The army sounds right. I remember Eddie watching some John Wayne war movies and saying that maybe one day he'd like to join the army. Really liked tanks and the big stuff, I remember."

Leo sighed. "It's just tough not knowing. We keep hoping for a letter, a call, maybe a card at Christmas, but nothing. It wouldn't be that bad but with Bernie the way she is, we'd like that he get in some sort of contact, you know, so he'd know. I don't expect him to come back and see us — her — but he should be told, don't you think?"

Albert nodded and asked tentatively, "So how's Bernie doing?"

Leo's eyes snapped back to reality. "Bernie," he said with a shrug. "She has her good days and all."

"She looks pretty good even though she's sleeping."

"Yeah, today's a good day. That's the only way to handle something like this, one day at a time. She can't think too much about the future, you know considering, so we focus on little things, little achievements, like making it in time for spring. That was her first success for the year. And not her latest success. Pretty much the big one for this year is today. She was so determined to make it to see me ordained. She's been talking about little else lately."

Albert raised his eyebrows in surprise. "Bernie's going to be coming to the church tonight?"

Leo shook his head. "No, she won't make it. The doctors said it would be too difficult on her body if we move her, so she's going to stay here. Her sister Delores is going to stay with her while I'm at the church and then we're going to have Delores' kid Mike videotape everything with his camera and watch it later. It's not the same as her being in the church, but the main thing is that she's still here on this earth with us when I get this done. That's the main thing. She would have been really disappointed if she hadn't made it to today. This thing is probably more important to her than to me. It's been her reason for . . . " Leo trailed off, his voice just getting quieter until it disappeared. He rubbed his chin and mouth with his hands and for several seconds seemed to have forgotten Albert was in the room. Albert sighed and reached out for his brother with his left arm and then slowly pulled it back, nestling his hand on the bed by his thigh. He paused for a second and then said,

"Well, I'm proud of you Leo. You're making us Apetagons look good."

Leo looked up at Albert and smiled softly, not showing any teeth but generating a warmth in his face. "Thanks Albert. I'm really glad you made the trip. I know things have been hard on you lately so I really appreciate you coming all this way." Leo reached out his right hand and almost touched his brother on the shoulder but slowly pulled it back. For a second, they made eye contact, and then it broke. Each away, trying to find something in the room to focus on. Two feet separated the two brothers as they sat on the face of Jesus.

5

"When our European ancestors first came to this area, they had already traveled for more than six months, crossing the Atlantic from the Shetland Islands, across to Iceland, Greenland and then over what we now call Quebec and into Hudson's Bay. The ships they travelled in those days were nothing like the ships we've got today. Mostly, they were made of wood and they had no engines, so they had to sail all the way. And those ships were small, a couple of hundred feet long, barely longer than the average hockey rink. The conditions must have been horrible, all those people cramped into that small, cold wet space, barely enough food to last the whole trip and everything they owned, all their possessions probably, strapped to their back. It must have been an arduous journey, a feat of exhausting difficultly. We can try to imagine what it was like, we can read all the books and the diaries of those who took part in that journey, but there's no way anyone of us here can imagine what it was actually like. They must have had their reasons for doing something like that, and they must have been pretty good because if someone in this group here today would come up to me and say, 'Hey Leo. Let's take only what we can carry on our backs and climb aboard this old rickety ship and head across the ocean to a country that we don't know anything about and see if we can actually make some type of future in this unknown land, I'd probably laugh in your face and call you crazy. No. Let me rephrase that. I *would* laugh in your face and call you crazy. I'd call Constable McColl over and see if there was any way he could have you committed."

A slight chuckle rattled through the congregation, and Leo gave it just enough time to filter through the crowd, then continued his sermon. "I bet that there were some people who *did* laugh in our ancestors' faces, called them crazy, and I bet right now there's some descendant sitting in his warm home on the Shetland Islands wondering what ever happen to that group, all those crazy McLeods, Apetagons, Arthursons, Sinclairs and the rest that left a couple hundred years ago." Leo pulled his hands from underneath his robes with a flourish and placed them on the podium. "Well, our crazy ancestors managed to make it to York Factory, and when they finally got off the boat, frozen, hungry and stunned by how far from home they were, they must have thanked the Lord for keeping them alive during their voyage. Nothing personal and I'm glad you all came down to the church for tonight's ceremony, but people back then were a little more religious than they

are now. God was a major force in their lives; he
controlled the winds that powered the sails and ensured
the icebergs slipped past their ships as they sailed
through the Arctic. It was God's will that they managed
to survive and they thanked God for keeping them safe.

"And when they finally caught their breath and
regained their strength at York Factory, they probably
prayed to God to keep them safe on the rest of their
journey. Because you see and as most of you know, the
ocean voyage was only the first half of our ancestors'
journey. They still had half a continent to cross because
they were hoping to travel down the Nelson and the
Saskatchewan to settle somewhere between Prince
Albert and Edmonton. Word had gotten back to the
Shetland Islands that there was plenty of empty land
for farming and our ancestors were hoping to start new
lives in this huge new land. But then Jake McLeod broke
his arm and the whole thing stopped. We all know that
some of the original group wanted to keep going, to
push on further to at least Grand Rapids or further west
before winter set in. But everybody figured that since
Jake McLeod was a key member of the group and had
made the trip this far, they could stop at this little
outpost for the winter and then make their way west,
when spring came.

"Back then, Norway House was only a small settlement, a few houses, the Hudson Bay post and the
Swampy Cree camped along the river. With all the trees
around the place, they figured they could build some
quick houses to make it through the winter, and there
was probably enough fish in the water and deer in the
woods so there would be enough food. The winter was

pretty bad, but remember these people came from the Shetland Islands so they were used to hard weather. At least it didn't rain all the time, and with all the snow piled up on the houses, it kept things even warmer. And they found that there was a lot of fish in the water and a lot of animals in the woods and the Hudson Bay guys were quite willing to pay them good money for any pelts they brought in. And the locals were also friendly too," Leo winked, "if you know what I'm talking about, and when spring came around, new families were sprouting up or were on their way. Our ancestors, probably still tired from their long ocean voyage, saw Jake McLeod's broken arm as a sign from God. The bounty of the land and the success over the winter showed that their journey was over and they could start to build new lives here in this community that we all now live in."

Leo took a deep breath, pausing enough in his story to let the congregation know that this break was only for them to take in what he had said and he still had some more things to say. There were a couple of coughs but little other noise. Leo exhaled, took in another breath, and continued.

"Every time I hear the story of how Norway House became a community I always think: 'Those people must have been giants.' For them to leave their homes to travel so far with so little, across the North Atlantic on a sailing ship almost two hundred years ago, they must have been giants. They must have had incredible strength, the strength of many men, simply to have undertaken such a journey. They must've had complete faith in God, faith that even I can't understand, to believe that such a venture would succeed. All my life,

I have thought that our ancestors must have been great men. They had to have been giants.

"But whenever I see the old homes that these people have built or come into this church that was rebuilt years ago to match the size of the original church built on this site, you can see that these people were not giants. If they were giants, then there was no way they could fit all of them into such a tiny space. They weren't great men of great strength, they were just men, men like you, men like me, people who may have undertaken an amazing journey, but they didn't really see it as such. They just wanted to live their lives as best as they could and when they came here, that's exactly what they did. Their journey was great, but so was they way they built this community. And they build this community with the simple actions of living their lives as best as they could. Because that is where greatness comes. Greatness doesn't come in great deeds or in great journeys across great distances but in how we all live our lives. Our lives are great not because we do great things but because we do the simple things. Our lives are great simply because we live them the best way we know how."

Leo paused, then said: "Would you now turn to page 124 for Hymn 347."

6

Albert, Sol and Bud stood outside the church. The church was a small and simple structure, a rectangular building topped by a slight A-frame and capped on one end, the south side of the building, by a steeple thrusting into the sky like praying hands. The church sat parallel to Playgreen Lake, at the edge of a peninsula on a rise about twenty feet above the shoreline. On the east side of the church was a gravel parking lot, spotted with a few trucks, one belonging to Sol Jacks. The road at the far edge of the lot led away from the lake, down the length of the thin peninsula, towards the centre of Rossland, the largest of the two communities that made up the Norway House Cree Nation. On the west side of the church was a cenotaph, the concrete corroding and blanketed by bird shit, the names of local boys who had fallen in the two World Wars and Korea faded and bleached by wind and rain, snow and fog. A well-manicured lawn surrounded the cenotaph and the grass almost stretched to the edge of the lake, but a long rift of reeds stopped it short.

Albert, Sol and Bud stood on the west side of the church, watching the lake. A breeze swept gently across the water, lifting up a few whitecaps to sparkle in the sun and setting the thrust of reeds to rustle and whistle.

"Hell of a sermon," Sol said, smoking a cigarette. The smoke whirled around their heads for a bit and then drifted away in the breeze. "So much better than last night. I was expecting more out of his ordination, it being a special ceremony, but I guess I was wrong."

"You'd figured they'd let him speak at his own ordination," said Bud. "That's what I was expecting to happen. That Leo would have the chance to give the sermon at his own ordination instead of having the Bishop bore the hell out of us with his opinions on whatever he was talking about. Christ, if Leo had given today's sermon yesterday, he would have blown that Bishop away."

Albert squinted into the sun. "As Leo told me, the way it works is that for the ordination, the Bishop is the one performing the service, so even though someone's becoming a Minister, the Bishop is the one who gets the chance to speak. Leo's first chance to give a sermon would only come when he was performing the service, which is what happened tonight. That's why he asked us to stay another day, because this service, being his first as a Minister, was probably more important than the actual ordination."

Sol took a final puff from his cigarette, tossed the butt to the grass and ground it out underneath his shoe. "Well, like I said, Leo gave a hell of a sermon. I don't remember a lot of sermons when I was a kid in church, but that was probably the best one I ever heard. He must have been working on that for a long time, just to get it right."

"It makes sense, eh, first time out you want to get it right," Bud said.

"Well, he started off his church career with a bang, I'll tell you that," replied Sol. "It's going to take him a lot of work if he wants to keep that kind of momentum going."

"He's got the voice for it," Albert said. "When Leo was a kid, he could out-talk anybody. He'd babble on for hours and hours if we didn't do anything to shut him up. Bill and I used to tie him to a tree when we were kids and leave him in the woods for a bit, but he'd still talk and talk. Once we thought about dropping him in the pit under the outhouse, but we figured we'd all have to go sometime and the last thing we wanted to hear when we're taking a shit is Leo talking up your ass. Then Bill came up with the idea of sending him on stupid errands — Mrs. Davids needs someone to clear up her yard, or fix her boat engine, stuff like that — and Leo would always head off to do his errand, talking all the time as he walked away. Strange thing was that Leo would always talk whoever we sent him to into letting him do whatever errand we sent him on. The only thing that could shut him up was Mom. One mean look from her and he'd shut up for good. If he didn't, she'd smack him across the head. If he cried, she'd smack him harder and keep on smacking him until he shut up. Best way to get Leo to shut up was just to tell him Mom was coming. He'd take off and we wouldn't see him for hours."

Albert blinked away the sun from his eyes and turned to the church. "I wonder if he knows we're still out here waiting. I hope he didn't take off with us sitting out here. It wouldn't be good to leave town without saying goodbye."

Bud peeked around the corner at the church, checking out the parking lot. "His truck's still there."

"Probably still inside cleaning things up or whatever it is ministers do after the service." Sol tilted his head in the direction of the church. "Go on and check him out, Albert. Bud and I will wait out here."

Albert nodded and walked around to the east side of the church where the main entrance was. He stepped into the building, the whistle and rustling of the breeze disappearing into the silence of the empty church. The building seemed a lot smaller than it did several minutes ago when every pew was filled and Leo was leading them in prayer. The church seemed melancholy, a lonely old man whose grandchildren have just left after their weekly visit. Even though he had just been a part of the congregation, Albert felt like he was trespassing, entering a forbidden place. He thought about calling Leo's name, but he felt that just whispering would somehow be considered sacrilege. He tiptoed slowly because even the echoing of his footsteps seemed out of place.

Albert walked softly up the centre aisle to the front altar. He knew there was a small room, a place where things were prepared prior to the service, and that Leo was probably in that room, wrapping things up. But he had difficulty taking the one step up to the altar and crossing it so he could find his brother. He knew it was a simple movement to get to the room, but there was something that told him he didn't belong there, not on the altar nor in the church. He waited for several minutes, trying to build up the courage to just take that first step and finally, even though he didn't have to, he crossed himself, looked up at the cross for forgiveness and stepped up to the altar, his feet silent on the soft carpet, and peeked into the room. At first he didn't see his brother. There was just a small noise, a soft, murmuring sound, like magpies cooing when they build their nests. And then he saw Leo.

Leo was sitting on the floor, still dressed in his bright formal robes, knees pulled up to his chest, feet crossed and his hands on his face. His body shuddered, and it took Albert a second to realize that Leo was whimpering. As he watched his brother, Albert had no idea what to do. He wondered if he should go to him. He had no idea whether Leo's tears were due to joy or sadness. And so he didn't know whether to join Leo in his celebration or comfort him in his difficult time. Albert had no idea how he could show his little brother that his bigger brother was there for him. At fourteen, Albert had left home to work, leaving ten-year-old Leo alone to deal with their mother and her constant outbursts of anger and violence. Back then, he was just glad to be finally free of the old bat and didn't really care how Leo would do. He just figured that Leo would do just like the rest of the family did, they would adjust. But Leo was left alone with their mother for four years, until he turned fourteen and was ready to go to work. After Albert took over Jerry Harrison's cabin, he finally realized that somebody should have at least checked up on Leo once in a while to see if he was all right. But in their haste to leave, Leo had been left behind with a crazy woman with nobody to protect him, and Albert had always felt guilty about that.

Albert decided finally to back away, to leave Leo alone. He figured that Leo had chosen this time, right after performing his first service and giving his first sermon, and this place, a room off-limits to everybody except him, to mourn for all the things he needed to mourn. He had plenty to cry about. His only son had run away, never to be heard from again except through rumours that may or may not be true. And the reason why his Eddie had run away was to get away from his always drunk and angry parents. Albert knew that Leo had always blamed himself for Eddie's disappearance, and rightly so. What kid would stay around with Leo and Bernice when they were at their worst?

Leo was also mourning the impending loss of his wife. With Bernice sick, it was up to him to keep the house moving as if there was nothing really unusual. Leo had created an amazing atmosphere and place for Bernice to live her final days, but in return had deprived himself of solace. Which was why his bedroom was so stark.

Then again, Leo could be crying tears of joy. His little brother was a smart man and the one thing that living with their mother had probably taught him was how to survive. Leo was someone who knew how to take care of himself in difficult times. When Bernice died, he would be all alone, but before that happened, he had found a new home. Sitting in the back room of the church, alone and crying, could be Leo's first step in building a new home now that his old one was almost gone.

Albert retreated from the doorway and left the church. He shut the main door behind him so it wouldn't make any noise. When he got back to the west side of the building, Sol had lit up another cigarette. "Leo coming?" Sol asked.

Albert shook his head. "He's still a little busy. I figure it'll be a while before he's ready to come out so we might as well head home."

"You say goodbye to him?" Sol asked.

Albert took a deep breath, sucking in the air as it drifted off the lake. He nodded. "Yep. And I guess it's time to go home."

Sol gave him a funny look, checking to see if Albert was okay. "You sure?"

Albert nodded, knowing what Sol was asking him. He was asking Albert if he was prepared to head back to Grand Rapids and face going back onto the lake again. Ever since that dark night, Albert had not returned to the lake. There had still been a couple more weeks left in the season but he pulled in his lines. He just parked his boat and stayed at home the day after Fency died. Nobody asked why because they all thought they knew the reason. They knew part of it — Barry Fency — but they didn't know the whole story. Albert would never forget that dark night, but that didn't mean he had to keep holding it in his arms. Like his brother weeping in the back of church, Albert knew it was now time to move on. "Everything's all right," he said with a smile. "Let's go home."

FENCY'S BOY

1

Fency dreamt of fire, flames drifting towards him,
dancing in the air like apparitions, like angels of light.
It wasn't an unusual dream; he dreamt of fire at least
once a month and sometimes, when he felt stressed over
something, every night. He had become so used to his
dreams of fire that they weren't nightmares to him. They
were uncomfortable dreams, but no more annoying
than a persistent insect that couldn't be batted away.

Sometimes the fire dream was quick. He would be
standing or sitting in his old trailer in Norway House
watching TV and an instant later the room would erupt
in flames. No explosions, no blasts, just an instant
conflagration surrounding him. And then a second later,
he would be on fire. Flames engulfing his entire body
except for his head which would always stay clear. He
always had a few seconds in his dreams so that he could
look at the fire, watch it consume his clothes and then
his flesh. Sometimes he even had enough time to hold
up a hand and watch the flames flickering from his
fingertips. He could feel the heat of the flames, feel it
burning into skin as it peeled away from his body, but
the pain wasn't as intense as he remembered. It burned,
but it didn't have that searing quality, that blistery rage
that scorched a path across his chest and neck.

Sometimes, in this dream, if he moved his burning hand quickly enough, the fire would create a streak of light in the air, the same way those sparklers did when he was a kid.

And then he would wake up, sweating from the heat and gasping from oxygen deprivation. There rarely was smoke in his dreams, but the fire would suck all the oxygen from his lungs, leaving him breathless. It was never the heat and the pain that woke him up from a fire dream, it was always the slow depletion of air, his lungs gasping, trying to suck in as much air as possible, but it just slowly withered away until he was left in a vacuum, his body screaming for breath.

But his present dream wasn't quick and dirty; it was slow, almost agonizingly so. Instead of sitting in his trailer, he was standing outside of it, as he had the first time the fire got him. The sun was bright, a few bulbous white clouds wafted above and a slight breeze drifted around him. He could feel both cold and heat in the wind, as if he were floating in the lake, his head above the surface, cold in the exposed air, yet around his chest the water was warm, but deeper in the lake, near his feet, it was cold. And the currents drifted around him, bathing him in various levels of warmth and cold.

But he wasn't even close to the lake; he was more than 40 miles north of it, standing in the yard of his old trailer in Norway House. And floating towards him, dancing on the air, like apparitions, were the angels of fire. They started to circle, keeping at least two feet distance as they revolved around him, fervent electrons orbiting a nucleus. And then one darted at him, lighting like a fly on his arm, singeing the hair, and then jumping back to its original trajectory. Then another, a second, a third, every few seconds one of the fiery angels would surge at him and then back. And then they lingered on his skin, raising a welt or a small blister, but he didn't move. If he ran, they would chase after him, dive down his throat and consume his body. So he remained standing in that one spot as the flames got braver and braver, and after a while they clung to his body, searing his flesh, burning, it seemed, right through to the bone. And instead of several bits of flame, they soon joined together and became one, encircling his body in a vortex that became hotter and hotter. He forced himself to remain in that spot, fighting the urge to flee. His sweat evaporated as soon as it appeared and he could barely breathe because of the heat. He saw the river in the distance and thought that if he started running, he might be safe. He dismissed that thought immediately because running to the river might seem like the safe bet, but if he ran, the fire would swallow him whole, and if it didn't kill him, it would leave its mark on him forever. He tried holding his breath to keep the fire out, but it licked at his nose, enticing him to breathe. He sniffed once and the fire jumped at the opportunity and slipped in. His lungs exploded with heat, the intensity of the pain jerking him out of the dream.

He awoke with a start, sitting up quickly, gasping. His skin was slick with sweat and his heart hammered in his chest. Some word tried to escape from his throat but it was too parched, so all he could muster was a small hiccup.

Irma Keung, petite and thin, hair jet black and tied into a long ponytail, stuck her head around the corner, a look of concern on her long oval face, her nostrils flaring, her brown eyes wide and small mouth pursed into a frown. "Are you all right?"

Fency responded by roughly waving his arm at her, trying to dismiss her from the room. He tried to speak, but was overtaken by a fit of coughs that almost doubled him over.

Irma went to the bed and placed an arm around him. "My God, you're soaking."

Fency's coughing subsided slightly and he rolled his shoulders and twisted his torso to escape her grip. She pursued him, placing her hands on his shoulders to hold him place, so he pushed her away and swung his feet to the other side of the bed. She started to move towards him but he waved an arm behind him, motioning her away. He managed to sputter three words: "Glass . . . of . . . water."

"Oh!" Irma gasped, and dashed out of the room. By the time she got back, Fency felt his heart slowing and his lungs able to suck in the precious oxygen. Irma approached him, standing just off to the side. "Water." She held the glass at arm's-length toward him.

He looked. It took him a second to register what he was looking at. He took the glass and downed it quickly. He handed it back.

"More?" she asked. He shook his head.

For a few seconds she watched him, and then sat on the bed next to him, making sure to give him enough space. She reached out a hand, gingerly touching him on the shoulder. He flinched but she kept the hand on his shoulder, offering no caresses or petting but just a presence, a connection to another person. His shoulder relaxed under her touch.

"You all right?" she finally asked.

He nodded but didn't look at her. His head still drooped over, chin touching his chest.

"Another dream?" she asked. Again, he nodded.

"Same one as last time?"

"Different."

"Different?"

He nodded.

"I thought they were all different."

He shook his head. "They are, but they are all about fire. This one was just," he paused as he searched for the right word. "This one was more intense."

Irma took a deep breath, held it for a second or two and then slowly let it out. "You should talk to someone," she said plainly.

"Talk to someone? That's your answer? I should go ahead and talk to someone and these dreams will just go away?"

Irma shrugged.

"Who should I talk to? Some type of therapist?" He pronounced the word "therapist" as if it were vulgar.

"Doesn't have to be a therapist. It's obvious that makes you feel uncomfortable, but you should at least talk to someone."

"Like who? Who should I talk to?"

She shrugged again. "Well . . . you could always talk to me."

He looked at her, searching her face for any sort of deceit or to see if she was just clowning around. Sometimes he couldn't tell; she'd tell some story, claim she heard it on the radio or read it in the paper or somebody from town told her, and he'd listen intently, thinking it was true, and then she'd realize that he believed her. She'd give a little laugh, a light slap on the arm and say, "Silly. I'm just telling a story. It's not true." She'd then read the hurt on his face and apologize for making fun of him. The apology was always sincere, but the event would be repeated again a few months down the road.

His face must have betrayed his thoughts because she spoke. "I'm serious, really. If you want to talk to me about anything and I mean anything at all, I'm willing to listen. I won't judge you, think less of you and I promise . . . I promise . . . that I'll just listen and won't offer you any advice or suggestions or interrupt you until you finish what you have to say."

"But I talk to you all the time. I tell you everything about the dreams. Nobody knows anything about them, except for you." He touched her on the knee. "You're the only one I tell."

She placed her hand on his. "I'm not talking about the dreams. I'm glad you tell me about them, and I'm sure that speaking out loud about them, that when you verbally form the words to describe your dreams to me, helps you deal with them. It makes them less, I don't know, dangerous . . . "

"Dangerous?" he said, pulling his hand back.

She shrugged and shook her head. "Okay, maybe dangerous is the wrong word. I don't know, I'm not saying that your dreams are dangerous to you. There must be some reason for them, but I think that talking about them like you do with me makes them seem more manageable. It allows you to deal with the dream and then move on instead of dwelling on the subject all day."

He started to say something but she cut in before he had the chance. "But I'm not talking about your dreams. I'm talking about the cause of your dreams." She gently slid her finger down his neck to his chest, following the line where the scar tissue met with his unblemished skin. He watched her finger and then looked at her face. "I know it's a difficult subject to broach but it's always been the pink elephant in the room with you. Everybody knows it's there, you know it's there, and everybody wants to ask you about it but nobody ever does. It's holding you back; there's always like a big weight on you, anybody who knows you can see it. It's must be a big thing for you to hold in and I think if you actually talked about what happened, actually told someone, it doesn't even have to be me, but just somebody, even a stranger in a bar or something, it might help your dreams go away. Then again, your dreams might stay, but I think that if you told someone, anybody, just once, what happened, you'd feel a whole lot better, maybe not at first but in the long run. Just like your dreams, talking about it makes it less dangerous and this time I mean dangerous. You suffered through some kind of traumatic event, I can only imagine what you went through up there, but only you actually know what happened and if you tell someone, actually verbalize the situation, I know for sure the weight will be gone."

He took in every word she said; he didn't brush it off, or fade into another headspace while she spoke to him. He listened because she was right; she was always right. She knew everything there was to know about him, even things he didn't know. At barely twenty years old, she knew more about people and how they lived and dealt with things than anybody else, he knew. Even more than Albert, even more than Sol, who claimed that he knew everything there was to know about how people operated — how they ticked, he always called it. But compared to Irma, Sol was an ignoramus.

From experience, Fency knew she was right; she had convinced him to talk about his fire dreams and though it had been difficult at first, it made them less menacing to him. At first he was worried that he was just pawning them off on her, that he would weigh her down with his troubles, but she was like a colander — she accepted and listened to what he said and let it flow through her. She took the weight of his dreams and filtered it out so it wouldn't weigh on her. And it worked as she said it would. He no longer feared sleep and the possibility of the dreams that might come. He knew that they would come once in awhile, but he also knew that he had somebody to share them with.

His eyes misted over and he enveloped her in a deep, adoring hug. He wanted to feel every inch of her body, to pull as much of her into him as he could. He wanted them to be one but to remain as two separate entities. She hugged him back, squeezing as much as he did. He wanted to talk to her about it, ever since he met her; he knew that she was the one he should disclose the story to. But he didn't know what to say. He had no idea where to start.

2

It had been a Wednesday afternoon when Robin McLeod knocked on Fency's front door, commandeering his truck to evacuate some of the old folks out of their homes. The satellite dish had settled into one of its quieter moments and though the picture wobbled slightly, it was clear enough to see Bruce Willis take on those European terrorists. It was probably the fifth or six time Fency had seen the movie, but it was mindless and loud enough that he didn't have to think too much. The shoot-em-ups and explosions were just the thing he needed to let the hash settle into his brain. Bitsy promised the best chunk of hash in the province, a cool, slow rise with a long, drawn-out high without the paranoia of pot or the out of control stupor of booze. Hash was the only way to go. Fency had tried almost every kind of soft drug in his time. In elementary school, Bitsy had showed him how to suck in the scent from markers to get a little buzz. It worked, but it also gave a mean headache. Glue was the same, a much longer high, but also a worse headache. From there they progressed all the way to gasoline, holding in the fumes in a plastic bag and then sucking on it for about ten seconds to get that blinding rush for a few minutes. After that wore off, you let the fumes build up, and then did it again.

In Grade Seven, they moved on to booze, stealing from their parents half empty bottles of rye or taking a couple bottles of beer from a twelve pack. They rationed the booze by only drinking small amounts and then doing a quick set of wind sprints to get the blood flowing faster.

Then they discovered the sweet scent of pot, Jake Arthurson scoring a couple joints off his older brother. Then it was hash, hash oil, joints with rolled papers smeared in hash oil, and finally, Fency hit his limit with magic mushrooms. At first, he thought they had been ripped off, they were so dry and chewy, like eating a styrofoam cup. And when nothing happened for the first half hour, he was sure they were ripped off because they didn't feel a thing.

But then it hit him in the middle of a Q-Bert game in the grocery store. The spring-loaded video hero Qbert began to slow down. Soon it was almost slow motion and Fency could do anything he wanted and beat any level the game threw at him. Even when the boxes on the game board turned inside out, he had no trouble. He and Bitsy staggered out of the store, giggling like madmen, every sound, every word, every moment the funniest thing in the world. Finally, after an endless bout of the giggles, Fency made it home, snuck in the back door and slipped into his room. As he lay in bed, head against the wall, he thought that shrooms were the best invention of mankind. He couldn't wait to try them again. That is until he felt his head sink into the wall. He pulled his head out quickly, shook off the thought and then lay back down. After a second, the walls started to move around his skull and envelop his head. This time it was harder to break away, but with some effort he pulled himself out. He looked back at the wall and saw nothing, just the wall by his bed. He went back a third time, and as soon as his head touched the wall it started to eat him. Slowly, he sank in, the wall pushing past his hair, moving up to his ears. Fency struggled to break free, but the wall squeezed tight, trapping him and slowly pulling him deeper. He shook his entire body, trying to break free, and with a massive effort, he finally snapped out of the wall. He shook his head clear, rubbing the scalp where the wall had enveloped it. He looked back at the wall, but again there was nothing there. He gave it a quick slug and pushed his bed away from the wall. And for an extra precaution, he slept with his head at the foot of the bed. From then on, he realized that shrooms were his limit; he would never try them again, and he wouldn't progress past them.

Things like hash were fine. The high was nice and easy without any weirdness. Good hash for him, like Bitsy had promised, would soothe his mind and keep him high and mellow for as long as possible.

But then Robin McLeod, the band constable, banged on his door. Fency had set his blinds so that he could see out, but no one could see in. So he had seen McLeod climb out of the brown band cruiser, hitch up his utility belt and walk to the front door. Fency didn't respond to the banging, hoping McLeod would think he wasn't home and move on. The band constable wasn't buying it. He banged on the door again. "Open up, Fency. I know you're in there, I can hear the TV."

"Fuck you, McLeod!" Fency shouted at the door, not moving from his chair. "Whatever it is, I didn't do it! I've been here all day watching TV!"

"I don't give a shit what the hell you've been doing all day, I just need to borrow your truck!"

"What the fuck," Fency said to himself, and then slowly stood from his chair, the hash making him a little unsteady on his feet. He walked up to the door and flung it open.

Norway House Band Constable Robin McLeod was standing with his hands on his hips, looking like an angry school crossing guard. He was tall and thin, his brown uniform sagging off of his shoulders and hips. He wore a pair of aviator glasses that were barely held up by his long Pete Townsend-like nose. There was a smudge of a mustache above his lips and his jet black hair was tied into two long braids that draped underneath his brown stetson.

"What's up, Tonto?" Fency asked. The nickname had been given to the band constable by Bitsy, who once said that even though McLeod looked like the Lone Ranger with his uniform and sunglasses, he was still an Indian. "You can wear the mask and ride the white horse," Bitsy had said, "but you'll always be Tonto."

"Band says I gotta commandeer your truck, Fency," McLeod said firmly. "Fire's heading too close."

Fency stared at McLeod like he was crazy. "What the hell? What do you mean you're commandeering my truck?"

"Commandeer means I'm going to take — "

"I know what the fuck commandeering means, Tonto. You don't have to tell me what the word fucking means. But you can't have my truck."

McLeod pulled a piece of paper out of his pocket, unfolded it and held it out like he was a town crier making a proclamation. "The provincial government has officially declared a state of emergency for the

Norway House and Cross Lake areas. So this piece of paper means that I can commandeer" — he stretched the word out — "anything I deem necessary to help in this state of emergency. I've got some old people, Lanny Arthurson's uncle down the road and Mrs. Jensen over in Fort Island, that need to be evacuated, but they don't have any transportation and we need your truck to help them old people."

The buzz from the hash made Fency hazy so that he barely understood what McLeod was saying. "What the fuck? You can't have my truck."

McLeod slowly slid his other hand to his nightstick and snapped the paper. The noise jerked Fency slightly out of his haze. "Jesus, Fency. How much shit have you been smoking? There's a massive forest fire out of control and it's heading this way. So I don't need your fucking permission. Whether you like it or not, I'm taking your truck. Where are the keys?" McLeod moved his head back and forth trying to see inside the trailer.

Fency looked up at the sky, and what he had first thought were overcast clouds was actually thick grey smoke drifting from the southwest. His stoned mind recalled some sort of news story about a fire somewhere in the province, but he didn't think it was this close. He looked back to McLeod and the constable appeared to be preparing to shove him aside.

"You can have my truck," Fency said finally. "But I'm driving."

McLeod shook his head quickly. "You're way too stoned man. I can't have you driving the old people around with your head full of whatever. Besides, I already got a driver lined up." McLeod jerked his thumb over his shoulder. Slouched in the front seat of the cruiser, like an apathetic teenager, was Bitsy. He offered Fency a nonchalant wave. He was a small man, called Bitsy because of his height. His hair was long, but instead of braiding it like many of the other young Indian dudes in Norway House, Bitsy tied it into a ponytail and tucked it under a red Harley Davidson bandanna. Bitsy had worn that red bandanna for years and Fency figured that he wore it everywhere, even when he slept. Bitsy also always wore a tight black T-shirt that clung to his chest and showed off the strong definition of his pecs and abs. Fency sometimes wondered how Bitsy could get his arms through the sleeves because his biceps were huge, so huge that Bitsy could no longer place his hands on his hips. What Bitsy lacked in height, he made up for in strength. He could bench 250 several times without working at it and he ripped so many Winnipeg phone books in half, in order to impress people, that most of the bars from Grand Rapids to Thompson started keeping their phonebooks behind the bar. Bitsy also made up for his shortness with a quick temper. Many times a bar patron had found himself flat on his back with Bitsy sitting on his chest pummeling him for some sort of slight that only Bitsy had heard or noticed. From hanging around with Bitsy since they were kids, Fency knew that the best way to escape one of these rampages was to treat Bitsy like an angry bear and play dead. If you curled up in a ball and protected your vital parts, and let Bitsy belt you a few times without fighting back, he'd tire and back off. And if you avoided eye contact or repeating whatever you said to set him off or apologize by buying him a couple of free beers, he'd be your best friend again. Bitsy wasn't really much of a friend, but since he had known him almost all his life, Fency figured that had to count for something.

Fency could barely hold in the giggles when he saw Bitsy in the front seat of the car, and McLeod saying that he was his chosen driver. "Bitsy? That's your driver? Bitsy?"

"Found him walking 'cross the bridge, heading in this direction. Nobody else around, most of them either fighting the fire or getting their families out of town, heading towards Thompson. So I sort of deputized him to help out. I was going to get you to drive, but you look way too stoned for me."

Fency held his hands up. "No way I'm letting that fucker near my truck. Last time he was behind the wheel he almost drove us into the river. You're better off with me driving. I might be stoned but I sure as hell won't kill Arthur Arthurson while trying to save him."

McLeod refolded the paper and stuck it back in his pocket. His other hand left the nightstick and rubbed his chin. He looked back and forth between Bitsy and Fency, trying to make a decision. "I don't know," he said, stretching out the sentence into a long drawl.

"Jesus, McLeod! How many tickets have you given Bitsy in the last four years you've been band constable, huh? How many accidents has he been in? How many trucks has the band given him since he started driving because he's wrecked them or put them in the river. He might be an old friend, but there's no way I'd ever get into a vehicle, even a goddamn snowmobile, with him at the controls. Bitsy's a fucking menace."

McLeod nodded thoughtfully and then looked deep into Fency's eyes. His eyebrows lifted in concern. "Yeah, but how stoned are you? I'm supposed to help these people get to safety. Not fucking kill them."

"Better to have me driving than him. And I'm a better driver when I've got a little buzz going. Sharpen's my senses. You get back into your car and I'll get my keys." Before McLeod could protest, Fency turned back into the house and went to pick his keys up off the kitchen table.

"You'll follow me out?" McLeod asked in an unsure tone.

Fency grabbed his wallet and stuck it into his back pocket. He snatched his keys off the table, tossed them into the air and caught them. "Whatever you say, Tonto. You're the boss." He walked out the door and shut it behind him. "Let's go save some old folks from the big bad fire."

Arthur Arthurson lived in a trailer similar to Fency's about a half mile or so down the road. His trailer was neater than Fency's, a fresh coat of baby-blue paint glistened off of it, and the old man had laid down a small lawn of sod that wrapped around the entire trailer within a ten-foot radius. At the southwest corner of the trailer, the end that faced the river and caught the most sun, there was a collection of patio furniture, a round table and four chairs with a bright yellow umbrella to complete the ensemble. Directly west of the trailer, just before the trees, was a ten by ten foot garden, the rows neatly lined with bright green leaves of lettuce, stalks of beans and peas, and tomato plants encircled by round metal cages that let the tomato vines climb to the sky and allowed for the placement of plastic to protect the delicate plants from dew or early frost.

They parked the two vehicles in the gravel driveway, Fency being careful not to drive on the nicely trimmed grass. McLeod went up to the door and Fency followed. Bitsy sat in the front seat, looking bored.

"You coming?" Fency asked, but Bitsy shook his head. He didn't even make eye contact. He just fiddled with the cruiser's shotgun holder, trying to figure out how to unlock the thing to get the gun free. Fency shook his head and rolled his eyes, and by the time he caught up with McLeod, Arthur Arthurson had already responded to the knock and opened the door. The old man was probably about 80 or so. He was Lanny Arthurson's uncle and Lanny himself was near 60, so Arthur must have been at least twenty years older. But the man carried himself upright, like eight decades of living only made him stronger. He was slightly leaner than Fency remembered from the last time he saw him, but there was a sort of resilience in the way the old man opened the door. His hair was short, cut as if he were in the army, and it was still mostly black with only a few spots of grey on the temples. He had wrinkles but they didn't hang off of him, they just further defined the face. And he had a pair of shockingly blue eyes that seemed to glow even in the daylight.

"What can I do for you boys?" Arthurson's voice was strong and never wavered. Fency felt his body stiffen to attention at the sound.

"I'm sorry, Mister Arthurson, but we're evacuating people because of the fire." McLeod's voice cracked slightly as he spoke.

Arthurson looked up at the smoke drifting above them. "Not too far away is it? Could be a day, could be a week, depending on the wind."

"Yes sir, it's pretty close as far as I can tell," said McLeod. "That's why we're evacuating people. Everybody who's got a vehicle is pretty much on their way out, but those who don't . . . " For some reason, McLeod didn't finish the sentence, he just let it trail away. Fency didn't know why McLeod was acting so sheepish at this point, until Arthurson spoke up.

"You helped my nephew take my car away five years ago," Arthurson said sternly, sending a blend of red through McLeod's face. "Said my eyes were going and my reflexes were getting slow and that I was posing a danger to myself and the general public." McLeod seemed to get smaller as the old man seemed to grow larger.

"Bunch of assholes," said the old man, and after an awkward couple of seconds in which Fency thought McLeod would start crying and begging forgiveness, Arthur Arthurson moved on. "Okay, guess we better get going before the fire gets here."

McLeod breathed a sigh of relief as the old man moved from the past. "Yes sir. If you gather some belongings we can get you a lift to a safer area."

Arthurson waved a hand to stop McLeod from talking. "Yeah, yeah. Just a minute." The old man stepped back into the house, letting the screen door close. Less than 30 seconds later, Arthurson was back, a windbreaker around his shoulders, a ball cap on his head and a small suitcase in his hand. Fency and McLeod looked at the suitcase and Arthurson answered the question they were both asking in their heads. "I've been packed like this ever since I heard about the fire a couple weeks ago. Can never be too careful, best to be prepared when something like this happens. Had the boat all ready to go just in case nobody showed up." He gave McLeod another stern look. "Guess I'm still okay to drive my boat." Arthurson walked briskly out of the trailer and towards the patio furniture. He set the suitcase on the grass, and with slow deliberation he folded up the umbrella and leaned the chairs against the table. This task completed he picked up his suitcase and looked at his garden. His whole body shivered in a deep sigh. "Shame about the tomatoes," he said. "It was going to be a good year for those."

Trying to be helpful, Fency said, "I can take care of them while you're gone, Mr. Arthurson. I just live down the road 'bout a half mile so it'll be no problem for me to check them out every day or so."

Arthurson looked at Fency for a few seconds and then chuckled. "Yeah, right. Thanks son, but if you think you can protect my little tomatoes, you're mistaken. This fire is the biggest one I've ever seen and the only thing that will stop it will be a few days of solid rain. When it comes through here, it's going to come fast, like a tornado. Not even the river will slow this baby down."

McLeod had opened the back door of the cruiser and motioned for the old man to climb in. Arthurson refused with a wave and headed towards Fency's old grey pickup. "Never ridden in the back seat of a police car so I'm not about to start today. I'll go with my tomato savior," he said with a smile directed at Fency. Except for a few black spots, even Arthurson's teeth seemed to be in good shape. After tossing the suitcase into the back of the truck, Arthurson and Fency climbed into the cab. He backed out, giving McLeod enough room to get onto the road, and then followed the police cruiser to the next stop.

Mrs. Jensen's house was on Fort Island, across the Nelson, so they had to drive back up the road past Fency's trailer and across the bridge and down the other side. Fency tried to let the hash slide into the back of his mind, and focused as much as he could on the road and the cruiser in front of him. Sometime during the ride, Arthur Arthurson started a conversation.

"You're Fency's boy, aren't you?" He phrased the sentence as more of a statement than a question.

"What?" Fency didn't trust his driving enough to look at the old man and talk to him. He keep watching McLeod's cruiser through the cloud of dust it threw up. "What'd you say."

"Barry Fency. You're his boy."

Fency answered with a nod and an affirmative grunt.

"Figured so. You look a bit like him. Not too much mind you, which is pretty good, if you know what I mean, no offense. But there's probably more of your mother in there than your dad. Which is good."

Fency quickly turned to the old man. "You knew my mother!?" He jerked the wheel and the back end of the truck began to slide back and forth on the loose gravel. Fency fought the wheel, twisting it back and forth until he managed to straighten it out of the swerve. The old man's only reaction to the truck almost driving off the road was to stabilize himself by placing a hand on the dashboard. "And they said that *my* reflexes were going," said Arthurson. "If you can't talk and drive at the same time, boy, don't bother. Just keep us on the road."

After settling and letting his heart slow a bit, and keeping his eyes on the road and his hands firm on the steering wheel, Fency repeated his question about his mother.

Arthurson nodded. "Yeah, I knew her. Not as well as some people, we weren't close friends or anything because I've been old for a long time, but I knew her enough to say hi and ask her how her day was going. I guess she went to school with one of my grandnieces or something like that."

"What was she like?"

Arthurson looked over, checking to see if Fency was just humouring him to pass the time. "You weren't that young when she died?"

"I was about six? Something around there."

"How old are you now?"

"Twenty-two."

Arthurson whistled. "Jeez, was it that long ago? I thought she died barely ten years ago. When the time zips past so fast like that, I guess I must be getting too old."

"I have these images of her, you know," Fency started. "Her playing with me, her and Dad swimming in the river while I'm splashing on the shore, her cooking supper, making bannock. Used to love her bannock; it wasn't dry like some of the stuff they sell out there. But that's the things I remember, nothing too big because I was just a kid back then you know. There are some pictures too around the house. Stuff from the wedding, a bunch when she was a kid and maybe a few from later on, but I don't really remember much."

Arthurson seemed to think for a few seconds and finally said, "She was a nice lady."

Fency grunted, disappointed, "That's what everybody tells me. They don't tell me much else."

"Well, that's because she was a nice lady. Sorry if I can't fill in any other details for you, but that's what I remember about your mother. She would always smile when she saw me shopping at the Northern store. She'd ask me how my grandniece was doing in Winnipeg, even though she probably knew more about her than I did. I knew the two of them still kept in touch with each other so she was more up to date than I was, but she always asked me how she was doing anyway, just to be polite. She'd prod me with questions — 'I heard she's doing this, I heard she's doing that' — and then let me tell the story even though she knew the whole thing way before I did. And she'd always ask me if I needed help with anything, if I needed a ride or something. And she'd always invite me to come over sometime for tea and bannock with jam. You know your house just being down the road and all. We might have been a half mile apart but she still called me her neighbour. And she wasn't just being polite like some people were like, she really meant it when she invited me over, I could tell. I can't tell you much more than that, sorry. She was a nice lady and I felt sad when I heard she died. I even think I cried for a bit, can't remember but I think so."

"That's all right," Fency said with a soft nod. He let his grip loosen slightly on the steering wheel and continued to follow the cruiser. In his mind, he added a new vision of his mother to the few that he had: she was standing in the Northern store, smiling and talking to Arthur Arthurson and inviting him over for tea with bannock and jam. "Thanks," he said to the old man.

It took a while longer to get Mrs. Jensen out of her home. She was reluctant to leave and kept forgetting why the three men — McLeod, Fency and Arthurson — were in her home. The old man came along because he knew Mrs. Jensen better than anybody else and understood how to keep her focused on the task of getting ready to evacuate. Mrs. Jensen was a tall, stocky woman with bright white skin and long grey hair and even though her house wasn't on the reserve and she didn't look native, her mother or father probably were or had some native blood in them somewhere.

"Come on Mrs. Jensen, there's no need to clean up the bathroom," Arthurson said, taking the lady by the arm and guiding her into the front hallway.

Mrs. Jensen allowed herself to be steered out of the room, but kept looking back. "But I have guests over. I can't have them using a messy bathroom, can I?" Despite her size, her voice was soft and delicate, like a shy teenager.

"Your bathroom looks fine Mrs. Jensen," Arthurson said. "If my bathroom looked like that on a regular basis then I'd be a happy man. In fact, I'm tempted to hire you to come over once a week and give that room and the rest of my place a good going over."

Mrs. Jensen blushed. "You always had a way with the words, didn't you Arthur. No one could out-talk Arthur Arthurson. We used to say you could probably sell water to Hydro, you talked so smooth."

"That's kind of you, Mrs. Jensen. But we have to get you ready. You're going to have to leave your home for awhile. Maybe a couple of days, maybe a week. We don't know how long, but there's a forest fire coming and we can't have you staying here."

"That's right," said Mrs. Jensen. "We should evacuate. Just like we did a few years ago. Last time, the radio said there was a fire coming and my granddaughter and her husband came over to get me. I wonder why they didn't come now."

At the mention of the granddaughter, Fency too wondered why she didn't come over and take care of the old lady. He looked over to McLeod to see if he knew the answer to the question. But McLeod just shrugged, looking just as confused and helpless as Fency felt.

"Maybe she's gone on ahead," said Arthur Arthurson. "She's got a couple of kids don't she?"

"That's right. A boy and a girl," Mrs. Jensen said proudly. "I'm a great-grandmother."

"Well, you don't look it, Audrey," said Arthurson. "So that means she's probably had to evacuate her kids out and that's why they sent us over, isn't that right Constable McLeod." For a brief second, McLeod had no idea what to say until Arthurson and Fency both prompted him by raising their eyebrows.

"That's right," McLeod said in a slightly authoritative voice. "We've been assigned to take care of you, Mrs. Jensen."

"That's right. We're all here for you Audrey," said Arthurson. "So you're going to need some clothes and things for a couple of days. Nothing fancy, just pretend

you're going to Winnipeg for a couple of days and pick
your clothes for that trip."

"I should take my suitcase."

"Good idea, Audrey. Where do you keep it?"

Mrs. Jensen pointed towards the hall closet. "It should
be in there."

Fency and McLeod both made a move towards the
closet and bumped into each other. McLeod backed
away and frowned. He hitched up his belt, indicating he
was the one here on official capacity so he should be the
one to help. Fency shrugged and stepped back. McLeod
reached into the closet and pulled out a red leather
suitcase. Arthurson had steered Mrs. Jensen towards her
bedroom and McLeod followed. Fency stayed at the
door, listening to the conversation as they packed.

"I don't think you'll be needing any winter clothing,
Audrey. Weather report says it's going to be warm and
hot for the next couple of days," said Arthur Arthurson.
"That's right, some nice comfortable summer clothes
will do. Don't worry about folding them too much, and
there will probably be a place you can hang them. If not,
everybody's going to be in the same boat so I don't think
anybody's going to notice the wrinkles."

Fency looked out the front door and tried to get
Bitsy's attention. He was still fiddling with the shotgun
but looking bored out of his mind. Fency wasn't sure
what he was feeling. At first he didn't really want to help
the old people evacuate. He had more important things
to do. And where the hell were their families? Why
weren't they doing this? But after meeting old Arthur
Arthurson and seeing how Mrs. Jensen became
confused once her home life was disrupted, he didn't

mind helping. Sure, Arthur Arthurson probably didn't need much help, short of a ride to wherever they were evacuating him to, but since he had no family left living in the area, somebody had to do the job. And Fency figured that having three men along to help out Mrs. Jensen, even though only one was needed, probably gave her a sense of security with this sudden change in her life. Bitsy, sitting in the cruiser where he had been ever since this stuff started, didn't seem to care a bit. This was just some annoying disruption in his life and if he was being forced to go along, he'd be as useless as possible.

Fency turned away from his friend and looked at the front room of Mrs. Jensen's house. It was neat, as old people's homes are, with two armchairs and a couch — old fashioned and out of style but still in good condition — surrounding a round, formica coffee table. Only one of the chairs, which also had some unfinished knitting sitting on it, was actually in line with the TV. The TV, although decades old, looked like it was barely used. It wasn't dusty or dirty; it just seemed to be asleep. There were a couple of end tables and every inch of surface was covered with knick-knacks and picture frames with photos of children at various ages in their lives. Similar pictures were scattered along the walls. There was a slight smell in the room, a mix of medicine with baking, not altogether unpleasant. Driving up to the house, Fency had felt a little sad for Mrs. Jensen that she lived in this house by herself, but standing in the doorway, seeing all the family photos on the wall, the knitting on the chair, smelling the warm air and hearing Arthur Arthurson telling Mrs. Jensen that they would turn around while she packed her delicates, he didn't feel bad for her life at all. She may have been alone in this house, just like he was in his trailer, but her home was her world, a place where she knew where everything was, where every corner was a comfortable corner, and when she went to bed at night it was in the same bed she had been sleeping in for the past twenty or 30 years.

It would be a shame if the fire destroyed Mrs. Jensen's home. It would be a shame if it destroyed Arthur Arthurson's home, but the old man seemed to have already accepted that fate and was ready to move on. But if Mrs. Jensen's home was taken in the fire, Fency knew that he'd feel real pain. It would be a crime because she didn't deserve it.

Somewhere in the back of his mind, Fency thought, if somebody's home had to be destroyed in the fire, it should be his. Nobody, he knew, would miss it. He crossed the room and grabbed the knitting and a couple balls of yarn off the chair. Mrs. Jensen started to weep a bit when they brought her out of the house, so Fency handed her the knitting and the yarn. She gave him a bright smile and touched him gently on his forearm. "Thank you very much, young man," she whispered. "I need to get this sweater done before winter."

Arthur Arthurson nodded at Fency. "Where'd you find that?" he asked.

"On a chair in the living room," Fency said with a shrug. "Figured she'd need something to do."

"Mother taught you well." Arthurson gave Fency's shoulder a squeeze and then helped Mrs. Jensen climb into the back of the police cruiser. He tucked her in setting her suitcase on her lap. The old lady looked at her suitcase and clung to her knitting like it was her only possession in the world, but it seemed to settle her.

"I'd better go along with her," Arthurson said, so Bitsy got out of the front seat and went over to Fency's truck to casually lean against the hood. Arthur Arthurson said nothing at all as he climbed into the front seat, but gave Fency a wave once he settled in. McLeod walked around the front of his cruiser, but stood by the door.

"We're evacuating everyone so you follow us up the road, Fency, and they'll get you settled away at the community centre," the constable said.

Fency was about to nod in compliance, but Bitsy interrupted him. "You gotta let the boy pick up some of his gear if he's going to leave home for a few days."

The constable glanced at Bitsy and then to Fency. "That's right, Fency? You need to pick some things up for yourself?"

Fency didn't know what to do. He didn't really need much if he was going to crash at the community centre. He had his wallet and his truck and if he needed clothes, somebody would probably help him out. Bitsy was up to something, but he didn't know what. He wanted to look at Bitsy to see what kind of response he should make, but he knew that if he did that, McLeod would realize that something was up. Fency felt it was taking him forever to respond to the question, but figured he was still feeling the effects of the hash. Bitsy jumped in and saved him from making a fool of himself.

"Jeez, Tonto, of course he's got to pick up some things," Bitsy said, walking over to the passenger door of the truck. "You make him drive all over town to help these old folks get packed and evacuated, you should at least let him get his own stuff packed."

McLeod looked as if he was going to say something to make Fency and Bitsy follow him, but then looked at his cruiser with Mrs. Jensen in the back, and Arthur Arthurson keeping up a conversation to stop her from starting to weep. "All right. You were a big help, Fency," said the constable. "The least I can do is let you pick up some belongings. We don't know how long or bad this fire is going to be, so you'll need about a week's worth of things. Just the essentials and none of the stuff you've been smoking today. You leave that stuff behind."

Fency nodded and saw Bitsy give a sarcastic salute. McLeod frowned, climbed into the cruiser and started it up. From the corner of his eye, Fency could see Bitsy climbing into the passenger seat, smiling like a drooling dog, but he refused to look at him directly.

McLeod pulled the cruiser around and stopped next to Fency. "Don't take too long," he said with a point. "That fire's moving pretty fast so just get whatever you need and get out of there. I want to see you two at the community centre in less than a half hour. I don't want to come back and get you."

Fency shrugged and Bitsy shouted from his seat. "No worries, Tonto. We'll be there in a jiff." McLeod gave them one last hard look and then pulled away, his cruiser trailing a cloud of dust.

Fency was about to climb into the truck and head over to his house and pick up a few things, but then Bitsy jumped out. "Holy shit. I thought Tonto would never fucking leave." The big dog smile was still on his face.

"This is just too damn perfect. Let's get this over with and then head over the bridge."

Fency felt a wave of confusion come over him, especially as Bitsy started walking over to Mrs. Jensen's house. He stood in limbo, one foot raised to go into his truck. "What the . . . "

Bitsy turned and saw him frozen at the truck. "What the fuck you doing man?" he said frowning. "We only got a couple of minutes or so. Get your butt in gear."

"I thought we were going back to my house to get some of my stuff."

"Jesus, Fency. That's just the story I told Tonto so he'd let us alone."

"We're not getting my stuff?"

"Later, man. But first this is the perfect opportunity. After the old lady's house, we'll hit the old man's and then head back to yours."

It took a second to realize what Bitsy was talking about, but once he realized his friend's plan, Fency's head cleared up immediately. He jumped from the truck and chased Bitsy before he got to the front door of Mrs. Jensen's. He grabbed Bitsy by the shoulder and turned him around. "No no no. Bitsy. This is fucking insane."

"Insane? Are you crazy? This is as perfect as you can get. Man when Tonto came to my door and told me he needed my help to evacuate some old people, I almost told him to fuck off. But then the perfect idea hit me and I told Tonto, if he really needs help, he'll probably need Fency too and his truck."

"You sent McLeod out to me?"

"Sure! We needed your truck and then later we're going to need your boat."

"My boat? Why the fuck do we need the boat?"

"Shit, Fency. Did you smoke that entire chunk of hash in one sitting? There's a goddamn forest fire coming this way and we can't leave the stuff at your place or mine because it'll probably get burned. With the boat we can hop down the river to Norman's Landing and stash it there for a bit or even head out to Grand Rapids and stash the stuff out back of your old man's."

"Jesus, Bitsy. We can't take the old lady's stuff. We just helped her out."

"And that was damn nice of us. Nice touch with the knitting too. Looked like you really cared. But since her house is probably going to get burned in the fire no one except her is going to miss it. No one's going to know anything has gone missing so we got ourselves a perfect crime." Bitsy's face was so bright with glee it was almost blinding.

Fency increased his grip on Bitsy's arm. "I'm not going let you take her stuff."

Bitsy's smile wavered, but only slightly. "I'm not going to take all her stuff, just some of it. The good stuff. I'm going to leave some behind just in case the fire doesn't hit her house, so if she misses anything, everybody'll think that she lost it 'cause she's old."

"I'm not going to let you rob Mrs. Jensen. She's a nice old lady." Fency tried to pull his friend from the door, but Bitsy didn't move. His face was beginning to turn red.

"Goddamn it, Fency, what the hell's wrong with you? Let go of my fucking arm."

"No. Leave the old lady alone."

"I'm not hurting the old lady. I'm just going to take some of her shit. Let me fucking go." Bitsy struggled a bit but Fency held on.

"Let's go Bitsy," he snapped.

Bitsy offered a smile of appeasement. "Okay, so you don't have to rob the old lady. I'll do it by myself. I'll take all the responsibility if something goes wrong. You can still be the good guy in all of this. But I get all the loot. Everything for me, nothing for you. Just let me go."

"Forget it Bitsy. We're going," Fency said as hard as he could.

Bitsy didn't move. The smile of appeasement was gone and there was no expression on his face, just a slow increase in redness. He stared at Fency, his eyes getting colder and angrier. Fency knew that at any second Bitsy could explode, drive a fist into his face and start to beat the crap out of him. "Let go of my fucking arm," Bitsy said, almost whispering. Fency wasn't sure if he would be able to fight back if Bitsy attacked. In the end, he decided that if he tried to protect Mrs. Jensen's house from Bitsy, he'd lose the fight and Bitsy would steal whatever he wanted anyway. Fency waited a few seconds, until he thought Bitsy would hit him, and let go of the arm. He stormed to the truck. He climbed into the driver's seat, intent on leaving Bitsy behind, but when he reached for the keys, they weren't there. Bitsy, half-expecting him to react the way he did, had taken the keys with him.

True to his word, Bitsy didn't take all that much from Mrs. Jensen's house: some jewelry and her old TV. The jewelry was in his pocket, and after he loaded the TV into the back of the truck, he climbed into the driver's seat, started up the truck and drove away. In the passenger seat, Fency was fuming. He wanted to grab Bitsy by the shoulders and shake him until he agreed to give back the goods. He ran through various scenarios in his mind in which he would force Bitsy to return Mrs. Jensen's jewelry and apologize and say what a stupid jerk he was. He imagined he and Bitsy struggling on the ground, and him finally getting the upper hand. He imagined sucker punching Bitsy, kicking him in the groin, throwing dirt in his eyes, driving an elbow in his face, even using the tire iron in the truck box and swinging it into his friend's shoulder, incapacitating him. And as Bitsy drove out of Fort Island and across the bridge, over to Arthur Arthurson's house, and while he broke into the old man's house and ransacked the place, and while he loaded Arthurson's computer, TV and stereo into the back of the truck, Fency imagined countless scenarios, countless conversations, countless attacks and countless permutations of all the things he would do to Bitsy to get him to turn the truck around and return all the stuff he had stolen. In every scenario he imagined, he was the victor, the hero who saved the old folks' stuff.

But in reality, Fency did none of those things, and while he imagined the scenarios, he also chastised himself for doing nothing. And when one admonishing session ended, another imagined fight began. And then it too ended and he started to beat himself up for doing nothing.

"You're pretty quiet there," Bitsy said, driving the truck towards Fency's house. "Don't you got anything to say?" he added in a mocking tone.

Fency ignored Bitsy, stared out the window and started another I'll show you session. When the truck pulled into Fency's front yard, Bitsy said, "I'm going to take your boat. You can have the truck," and then climbed out, leaving the keys in the ignition. Fency watched as Bitsy started to carry the stuff over to the boat. He again imagined jumping his friend and tossing him into the river. But, finally, he gave up any plans to attack Bitsy. There was no way he could stop him. Bitsy would fight back and win. And instead of saving Mrs. Jensen's and Arthur Arthurson's stuff, he'd end up with a broken jaw or something like that.

Resigned, Fency slowly climbed out of the truck and went into his house. The TV was still on, the remote on the kitchen table, so he shut it off. He went into his bedroom, gathered up some clothes and started to stuff them into a plastic garbage bag. He wasn't even sure that when he showed up at the community centre he was going to report Bitsy to McLeod. As Fency searched for matching socks, he heard Bitsy come into his house. He knew Bitsy wouldn't take his TV — there was some sort of code about stealing from friends — so he didn't worry. "I need to use the can," Bitsy shouted out.

Fency shrugged to no one in particular and continued stuffing his things into the bag. When it could hold no more, he slung it over his shoulder and headed towards the front door. He was going to shout something to Bitsy, to tell him he was leaving, but saw the figure of Constable McLeod standing in the doorway.

"Hey Ton — " was all he got to say before McLeod burst into the trailer, his hand on his baton.

"I can't believe you'd do something like that Fency," McLeod said, his face filled with anger and disappointment. "I can't believe you'd actually rob Mrs. Jensen and old Arthur Arthurson just after evacuating them. I wasn't sure if you were up to something. I didn't think you were the type of guy to do something like that, but there you go. What you did is probably the most disgusting thing I've ever seen, stealing from your own people like that."

Fency dropped his plastic bag and held up his hands. "I didn't do anything, McLeod. I was just — "

"Shut up Fency. You make me fucking sick." McLeod held one hand on his baton and started to reach for the handcuffs that hung off his utility belt. "I don't want any trouble, you know you've been caught, so I want you to go peacefully. Turn around and let me get these cuffs on ya so I can take you in."

"I'm telling you McLeod, I didn't do anything, I wouldn't steal from those old folks, it was — "

"Didn't you hear me? I told you to shut the fuck up! I checked your boat and saw all the stuff in it!" McLeod screamed. He yanked his baton out of the holder and jabbed the end of it into Fency's shoulder. He took the blow, feeling the sharp pain. "Turn the fuck around and don't give me any trouble or I'll fucking wrap this thing around your head."

Fency waved his hands appeasingly. "All right. All right, McLeod," Fency said, turning away, facing the window over the kitchen sink. "I'm turning around. Put that fuckin' baton away."

McLeod jabbed him again, in the back, pushing him up against the kitchen counter. "Shut up Fency. You got no right to say anything." Fency heard the jingle of the handcuffs and turned to see McLeod set the baton on the kitchen table. When McLeod saw Fency looking at him, he slapped his face, the sting sending a flash into his eyes. "I said turn around," McLeod barked. He snapped one cuff onto Fency, locking the cuff tightly on the wrist so it dug into the skin and started to cut off his circulation.

"Fuck, that's tight."

"Shut up!" McLeod shouted, starting to lock the other cuff on. "Once I get you locked in I'll look for your part — "

Suddenly, there was a heavy thud, like someone dropped a frozen turkey. McLeod grunted and immediately dropped to the floor, leaving Fency with one hand cuffed. Fency turned around and saw Bitsy, holding the baton in his hand and smiling like it was Christmas. He smacked the baton once in his hand. "Surprise," he said. "Good thing I had to take a leak or Tonto here would have taken you in for something you didn't do."

Fency bent down to McLeod's prone body, noticing blood oozing from the back of his head. He touched the stickiness, but quickly pulled away. "Jesus, Bitsy. Did you have to hit him?"

"Couldn't let him take you in," Bitsy said with a laugh. "You're an innocent man."

"Shit, he's bleeding. He looks pretty bad."

"Naw, Tonto's got a hard head. He'll be all right. He'll have a headache for a week, but he's one tough Indian. He'll bounce back." Bitsy tossed the baton on the floor. "Well, I'm off. Thanks for the boat, Buddy," he said, slapping Fency on the shoulder. "I'll probably leave it in Grand Rapids so you can pick it up there. I won't be back for a few months, 'cause of this." He stepped over McLeod, pushed past Fency and went out the door. Fency looked at McLeod lying on the floor, saw the baton and started thinking about how easily Bitsy had attacked the constable and how he nonchalantly robbed Mrs. Jensen and Arthur Arthurson.

Enough! he thought. He had let Bitsy get away with a lot of things in his life, all those times picking fights in the bar, all those times he trashed Fency's trailer, all those dollars he quietly stole out of his wallet, all those . . . everything. For years Fency had thought that Bitsy was his friend and friends give other friends a bit of leeway every so often. But all this, stealing from Mrs. Jensen and Arthur Arthurson, belting McLeod on the head, probably killing him, and getting him mixed up in it, was way too much. For years, he'd thought Bitsy was a friend, but he now realized that he was just an asshole who didn't give a shit about anybody except himself.

Fency grabbed McLeod's baton and burst out of the trailer.

Bitsy was calmly walking down the path towards the boat. Fency chased after him. "Bitsy!" he shouted.

Bitsy stopped and turned. When he saw Fency coming towards him with the baton in his hand, he laughed.

"What the fuck you going to do Fency? You gonna stop me or something?"

Fency came within a few feet of Bitsy and stopped. "You've done enough."

Bitsy laughed. "Jesus, Fency, you gonna hit me with that thing or what."

"Whatever it takes."

"Don't be a fucking idiot, Fency. Turn around and get back to your truck and get the fuck out of here before you get yourself hurt."

"I'm not afraid of you, Bitsy."

"Sure you are," Bitsy said with a laugh. "If you weren't afraid of me you would have stopped me from robbing those old folks' houses. You wouldn't have kept thinking about what you were going to do to stop me, but actually done something to stop me. You probably would have gotten beat up but at least you would have tried."

Fency held the baton so Bitsy could see it. "That's what I'm doing now."

Bitsy shrugged and took a half step back. He set his feet shoulder width apart and gestured with his fingers for Fency to move forward. "Well. Come and get me."

Fency froze, not knowing what to do. Bitsy was right, he was frightened; even with a baton, it was barely a fair fight. Bitsy was much stronger, much faster, a whole lot meaner. He thought nothing of punching a total stranger in the face, just because he felt like it. Fency agonized for days even when he accidentally struck a squirrel or bird with his truck. Even after all that had happened today, he still couldn't bring himself to strike. He had to stop Bitsy, but he had no idea how.

"Come on you fucking chicken!" Bitsy shouted. "Let's get this over with!"

Fency held the baton up and took a quick step forward, but then stepped back. It was the indecision Bitsy was waiting for. He jumped forward, kicking Fency in the leg and swinging a right. Fency's thigh erupted into pain but he managed to deflect Bitsy's punch with his left. It glanced off the side of his head, but it still sent a burst of light and a shudder through his head. He felt a dull throb start to pulse in his ear. But the kick and punch were just Bitsy's ruse to distract Fency. While Fency deflected the punch with his left hand, Bitsy grabbed at the baton with his other hand. Fency shook himself out of the flash of the glancing blow and hung on. He would not let go of the baton. They struggled back and forth trying to wrest if free, Bitsy trying to kick at Fency while he dodged the blows. Bitsy yanked hard and almost pulled Fency off his feet; he caught his step in time and looked up just in time to see Bitsy thrusting his head forward in a head butt. Fency countered by jumping back, pulling Bitsy off balance. Bitsy staggered forward on his own and Fency's momentum, and tried to swing another punch. But that just put him further off balance, and with another yank, Fency pulled the baton free. He didn't think about what he would do next. He just instinctively swung the baton towards Bitsy, heard the crack as the heavy plastic connected with Bitsy's skull, felt the vibration of the blow shudder up through his shoulder, and saw Bitsy's eyes roll back in his head as he fell to the ground. Fency also fell, landing on his butt, exhausted.

Bitsy seemed so still that Fency thought he'd killed him. "Jesus Christ," he said, scrambling on his knees to check on his friend. He banged his knee into the baton. "Goddamn it," he shouted, grabbing the baton and hurling it over his shoulder. A second later, there was a small splash. "Bitsy. Are you all right?" Fency said, frantically feeling the body with his still handcuffed hand, searching for a pulse, checking to see if Bitsy was still breathing. He found a slight pulse on Bitsy's neck; it was fast, yet steady. A thin stream of blood ran down Bitsy's neck and Fency followed the trail with his hand, until he reached a tacky area just near the back of Bitsy's ear. He gently touched the wound and pulled his hand away. There wasn't as much blood on his hands as he expected, and he thought that maybe that was a sign that Bitsy wasn't too badly hurt. Fency fell onto his back, staring at the smoke from the fire drifting above him. There was a throbbing in his right wrist, the hand that yielded the baton, and a dull ache on the side of his head where Bitsy's first punch glanced off. The ringing in his ears was loud and steady, a whine that seemed to be getting louder. Fency brushed his ear with his hand, trying to drive the sound away, and accidentally spreading some of the blood on his hand against the side of his face. The sound dissipated in his left ear as he brushed it, but it was still present in his right ear. And getting louder.

Fency quickly realized that the sound was not coming from inside of his ear and jerked upright. The sound continued to increase in volume and it seemed like the gusting of wind, but with a deep roar, like a jet steadily gunning its engines for takeoff. Fency whirled around, looking for the sound, and on the other side of the river he saw the wall of flames advancing from the southeast. The fire first hit the top of the forest, scouts of flames leading the way like dancing explosions, randomly pouncing from tree to tree with only a second or two needed to destroy the leaves before leaping over to the next victim. The main body of the fire followed behind, an inferno, advancing like the tanks of a blitzkrieg, gorging on the forest, devouring everything and the roar drowning out all sound except for the irregular pops which were actually the trunks of trees snapping in the wake of the flames.

Fency wanted to scream — he would not have been able to hear himself — and he wanted to run, but the fire was too intoxicating. It was terrifying, destructive, yet beautiful. Within 30 seconds, it had moved more than 100 metres, directly across the river from him, swallowing the entire forest, mowing it down like the fiery hand of a god.

Even though it felt like he was standing in front of an oven, Fency figured he was safe on his side of the river, and was intent on watching the fire rage past him. But then one of the trees exploded, sending a stream of flame across the river to the island that split the Nelson in two. The burning wood landed in the dry weeds at the shore's edge and slowly started to eat away at the underbrush. Then one of those dancing explosions made a leap across the river and jumped on one of the trees. Within a few seconds, it had moved onto several other trees and had sparked several offspring.

Fency started to back away from the river and tripped over the prone body of Bitsy. He landed on his back, but the jarring of the fall jerked him out of his stupor. He leapt to his feet and ran to the truck to make an escape. He got halfway before he remembered Bitsy on the ground near the river and McLeod inside the trailer. It wouldn't be long before the fire made the leap across to this side of the river, and if he left them behind, they'd be dead. It took him another second to decide to first get McLeod out of the trailer and into the truck and then get Bitsy. Fency didn't know how he came to that decision — maybe because McLeod was lighter and probably easier to move, maybe not. But his first reaction was to go after McLeod.

Fency ran to the trailer, almost kicking in the door. He burst into the trailer shouting, "Fire! Fire!" with no idea why he was shouting. McLeod was still on his back, slowly regaining consciousness and moaning. Fency reached out and pulled the constable to his feet.

"What the . . . " McLeod slurred. Fency slipped one arm underneath McLeod, trying to balance the man and get his feet moving.

"Come on McLeod," he said gasping. "The fire's just across the river and it looks like it's about to jump over."

McLeod perked up a bit at the frantic sound of Fency's voice and tried to move his feet, but he was just too unsteady. Fency moved in front of McLeod and bent his shoulder into the man's stomach. "Hang on McLeod. Let me do all the work. Just hang on and I'll get us out of here."

Fency pulled McLeod's body over his shoulder in the classic fireman's carry, set his balance and then headed out the door. McLeod groaned heavily when Fency banged the constable's back to open the door.

"Sorry man," Fency said as he clumsily climbed down the steps. "Can't worry about being too careful. Fire's moving pretty fast so I have to get to the truck pretty quick. Then I'll get Bitsy and we'll get the fuck out of here."

Fency staggered under the weight of the constable, and before he got within ten feet of the truck he saw that the fire had already crossed the river ahead of him and was advancing further north. There was no way to escape using the truck. Fency whirled around, McLeod on his back, panicking, wondering what to do. Smoke filled the air, making it difficult to breathe and increasing his panic. His heart pounded and adrenaline set his system in high gear. He froze for several seconds, seeing the tops of the trees around him start to fall victim to the fire. One exploded nearby, sending a blaze of burning branches into the river.

"The boat!" Fency shouted, remembering Bitsy loading the loot from Mrs. Jensen's and Arthur Arthurson's homes. He got his bearings and pushed through the smoke, towards the river. Even though McLeod was heavy and starting to struggle, Fency didn't slow, and he managed to make it to the river. There was a bit of a break in the smoke over the river and Fency could see almost everything around him was in flames. The entire forest across the river, on the island, and up and down the shore was burning or in the path of the fire. Fency looked for the boat and saw it a few feet south of his point. He stepped across the rocks and jumped onto the tiny dock. He bent over and dropped McLeod in the boat. The constable started to babble, repeating "Oh my God. Oh my God." He stood up for a second, intent on stepping out of the boat, but Fency shoved him back down.

"Stay in the boat, Tonto," Fency said, but McLeod rose to his feet again.

"Oh my God. Oh my God. We're going to die. We're going to die," McLeod whimpered. He tried to get to his feet but Fency jumped off the dock into the river and held McLeod back. "If you get out of this boat then you're fucking dead. The fire's all around us and the only place we might be safe is on the river. Wait for me. I gotta get Bitsy."

McLeod seemed to get the message and stayed in the boat. "Oh my God. Oh my God . . . "

Fency ripped off his shirt, stuck it into the river and wrapped it around his head. He staggered out of the water, searching through the smoke for the path to the trailer. Bitsy couldn't have been too far, but he wasn't sure. The fire roared around him, deafening, the heavy black smoke filled his lungs, burning him from the inside out. Branches and trunks snapped all around, landing near him, but he pushed on. There were flames everywhere, but the wet shirt on his head and his wet jeans and boots gave him some protection. Still, he knew it wouldn't last. Already some of the flames started to lick at the skin on his torso, trying to set him on fire. A few blisters welled up painfully, but Fency knew that it took a lot of heat to set human flesh on fire. He also knew that he didn't have much time to find Bitsy, less than a minute or so before the fire would be too much and he would have to turn back.

Fency tripped over Bitsy crawling towards the trailer. Bitsy's shirt had been burned off of him and the skin on his back was black. Bitsy didn't seem to notice his collision with Fency and continued to crawl forward. Fency reached out and grabbed his friend underneath the shoulders and pulled him back. Bitsy fell back and allowed himself to be dragged for a few feet but struggled to break free.

"Come on Bitsy! You're going the wrong way!"

"Fuck off and let me alone!" Bitsy shouted, swinging backhanded. The blow knocked Fency into the burning grass and he screamed in pain. But he jumped to his feet and grabbed Bitsy again. He pulled with all the strength that he had left and started to drag Bitsy back, listening for McLeod's whimper to find the location of the boat. Bitsy kicked and screamed but Fency hung on and pulled as hard as he could. He could feel the river behind him and hear McLeod shouting.

"Hurry! Hurry! The fire's all around us!"

The flames burned Fency's back and the smoke sucked out all the oxygen but Fency kept pulling the struggling Bitsy. But he slipped on a wet rock and fell back against the dock. Bitsy broke free and started to crawl away. Fency jumped to his feet, "Jesus, Bitsy you're going the wrong way!" and made a grab for his friend.

While Fency was struggling with Bitsy, the fire had consumed the trailer and was heating up the propane tank. Finally, as Fency reached out for his friend, the tank exploded, sending an eruption of flame that hit Fency dead centre in his chest and blasted him into the middle of the river. He didn't feel the hot gas searing his chest or the cold slap of the water as he landed in the river. He didn't hear the other explosions around him, the further snapping of trees or the rocket-like roar as the full force of the fire swept past.

He only remembered the sound of a boat engine and the soft hands of Constable McLeod pulling him out of the water and setting him on the bottom of the boat. Fency was too much in shock to feel the pain of his burns and looked up at McLeod, who was hunched over in the boat with one hand holding a wet rag on his face and the other gripping the steering handle of the engine, guiding them to wherever.

"Where we going?" Fency managed to ask. His throat erupted in agony as he spoke.

"South. Towards the lake. Fire's already been through there so it should be safer . . . I hope," McLeod said, jerking his head to point their direction. "Thanks for getting me out. I owe you my life." He pulled the wet rag from his face and placed it onto Fency's mouth. The coolness offered a bit of solace but it was still difficult to breathe. "Don't try to speak or breathe too deep. Smoke's a real bitch." McLeod grabbed another rag, dragged it in the river and then held it against his mouth.

Fency stared up at the sky, the glow of the flames on either side of the river reflecting off the smoke. There was only one thing going through his mind. He pulled the rag off his face, and even though it was one of the most painful things in the world, he spoke. "Bitsy?"

McLeod looked down at him, no expression on his face. He removed his rag. "Forget about Bitsy. You tried to help, but . . . well, that's Bitsy for you. At least you tried."

McLeod returned his wet rag to his mouth and motioned for Fency to do the same. Fency did, but didn't think it would help. He just saw the fire and smoke all around him and wondered if he would ever escape it.

GRAND RAPIDS

1

Albert stepped into the central hallway of the Esso station. To his immediate left was the convenience store where you paid for your gas. The convenience store offered any type of junk food, some pharmaceutical items, the *Winnipeg Free Press*, the *Globe & Mail* and numerous magazines, videos for rent, milk, bread and other basic amenities, maps, directions, some T-shirts, ballcaps, and postcards as souvenirs, 6-49, Super Seven and scratch-and-win lottery tickets of all types, cigarettes, tobacco (smoking and chewing), rolling papers, child-proof lighters and the cashing of personal cheques — approved town residents mostly but sometimes visitors with two pieces of government ID and/or a major credit card.

Like the bar, there was a glassed-in area just inside the entrance of the store. The register and the safe sat in the glass box and Keung always kept one person, usually his wife, his sister-in-law or himself locked in that glass box while the station was open. You paid for your purchases through the tiny slot in the front. Sol Jacks once asked Keung why he installed the bulletproof security glass when in the entire history of the town, there had never been a single hold up, let alone one with guns.

"You probably think I'm crazy, don't you Sol. Old Keung just a little paranoid, to be afraid that someone try to rob my family."

"Yeah a little, especially when nobody in town's ever thought about robbing you."

"It's not you or anybody in town I'm worried about Sol. It's these damn Americans, coming up with their trucks and their guns."

"They're hunters Keung. They come up here to go hunting because they don't have any animals left at home. So they come up and kill ours and buy our gas and food."

"You must think I'm really stupid don't you Sol. I know they're hunters. But they're American hunters. And they like to drink when they hunt and sometimes they don't usually get what they want and they come back drunk and angry. With guns in their trucks."

"But it's never happened before. No American hunter has ever come into town so pissed off to take a potshot. Maybe a fight or two at the bar but no gunplay."

"I can't take that chance. Especially since they're Americans," Keung said, and the argument was over. The glass was in, and after three years, everybody got used to it.

On the wall directly in front of Albert, between the two washrooms, a bulletin board hung. Notices written on various types of paper, foolscap, bond, cardboard, construction and even some post-dated envelopes, covered the board like makeshift wallpaper. Most of the notices were small personal offerings, services — babysitting, mechanical, construction or things for sale — a boat, cars, old furniture, stereo equipment and some old baby clothes and items. But tacked to the board on the lower right corner, an 11x17 poster, the Band's name along with Manitoba Hydro's logo, a stubby upside down trident forming the letter M across the top, was the announcement of the meeting.

GRAND RAPIDS GENERATING STATION
UPGRADE PROJECT INFORMATION MEETING
IMPACT BENEFIT AGREEMENT
GRAND RAPIDS COMMUNITY HALL
AUGUST 8
8 PM
ALL TOWNSPEOPLE, EVEN THOSE WITHOUT
TREATY CARDS ARE ADVISED TO ATTEND THIS
EXTREMELY IMPORTANT MEETING!

PLEASE ATTEND!
YOUR FUTURE IS IMPORTANT!

Albert checked his watch — at least four hours before the meeting — and then turned to his right to go into the restaurant. The restaurant offered all types of diner-style food from breakfast (anytime) to the soup and sandwich special of the day at lunch and the dinner special complete with your choice of soup of the day or salad, one regular soft drink or refillable coffee, a bun, and for dessert, a choice of one slice of cake or pie or a bowl of ice cream, jello or pudding. There was also a menu of Chinese food items, mostly deep fried and breaded and offered with sweet and sour or plum sauce, Minute rice and a plastic-wrapped fortune cookie for every person in the party, whether they had eaten Chinese food or not. Some of the restaurant's customers were American fishermen heading further north for better catches, or hunters during hunting season heading the same way, or summer weekend campers heading for one of the provincial parks. The majority were business travelers, salesman or company reps and/or truck drivers heading north with calls and deliveries, or south back home to Winnipeg. And of course there were the 15-30 passengers, depending on the day and the time, from the bus that used the Esso as a 30-minute stop on its six daily trips, three north and three south, between Winnipeg and Thompson and towns in between.

The restaurant held fourteen identical square formica-topped tables with stainless steel legs. Each one was encircled by four identical brown vinyl chairs with matching stainless steel legs. Four tables ran along the front window, with another four along the far perpendicular wall. The remaining six tables lined up in two rows of three in the centre of the restaurant, the rows separated by a barrier of wood and formica that extended six inches above the top of the tables.

Except for a lone trucker seated at the second table from the door, his back to Albert and hunched over a coffee and a newspaper, the restaurant was empty. Albert walked through the restaurant to the table at the far back corner. A half empty coffee cup and an ashtray full of used butts sat in the centre of the table. Albert sat down on the chair with the view of the entire restaurant in front of him and shut his eyes. His brain drifted off but a connection to his senses lingered. The hum of the lights, the scent of frying oil, the coolness of the vinyl chair against his back. The hard scrape of a chair against the floor and the clatter of change hitting a table: the trucker's break was over. Albert heard the trucker's boots walk across the floor and then another set of footsteps, lighter and coming from the kitchen area.

Then the trucker's voice, a gruff grunt: "See ya."

In return, a female voice, low and gravelly. "Have a good ride home, Bill."

"Thanks Elaine." And the trucker was gone. The light footsteps returned to the kitchen. About a minute or so later, Albert heard a diesel tractor unit start up, shift into gear and pull out of the parking lot. Albert drifted off, hearing the trucker's voice again and again — "Thanks Elaine" — and thought about the first time he heard that name.

40 YEARS AGO

A heavy humidity drifted throughout the hall as the band began another tune, some country number popular on the North Dakota station that the locals' radios could pick up on a calm Sunday, the signals using the still water of the lake or the ice in the winter as some type of booster signal. A cheer went up in the crowd and the old community hall started to shake to the rhythm of the men's weekday workboots dancing on a Saturday night. The vibrations started shaking all the ashtrays, glasses and bottles on the tables so that they provided another cadence about half a beat or so behind the popular song. Some voices sang along to the entire song and almost everyone sang the well-known chorus.

Albert enjoyed the music. He loved how the catchy melody would stick in his head so that when he was out running his traps, he'd catch himself whistling or humming the song. He also enjoyed the cheerful rhythm that got his head nodding or his toes tapping, but he always stayed away from the dance floor, away from the heat and the noise, preferring to lean quietly against a back wall, nursing a drink or two for the entire night. For the most of the night, he'd be alone except for the times when the band took a break. Then Barings, his face red and beaded with sweat, would come over and stand next to him. Albert thanked the lord that Barings smoked because the heavy rank of BO would vent off of him like mist off the lake. Albert didn't really like the smoke — he was never a fan of the habit — but he'd rather smell smoke than Barings' particular brand of musk.

"Man, Albert. I don't know how you can stand here all night when there's all these great women and great music," Barings said out of breath. "You gotta get up dancing. You have no idea what you're missing out there."

"I'm all right. I like it back here."

"But Albert, you're not going to meet someone if you stand out here all night."

"Who says I'm here to meet someone."

Barings laughed loudly, spraying Albert slightly with spittle and sweat. "Shit Albert, that's the only reason why people come to these things. You think we're all here just because we like dancing?"

Albert looked Barings up and down. "You sure look like you like dancing. You're on the dance floor all the time, sweating so much you could flood that dam they're talking about building."

"But I'm not dancing by myself am I? I'm dancing with somebody and if she likes the way I dance, then we get to talking and if she likes the way I talk, then you know." Barings began to blush. "Then we might be getting to some other stuff."

Albert chuckled. "Then why the hell are you here talking to me instead of talking to your dance partner of the last half hour. Didn't she like your dancing?"

"She liked my dancing just fine. I just came over to see how you're doing."

Albert slapped a friendly hand on Barings' shoulder but instantly regretted it. Barings' shirt was cold and clammy from all the sweat. He pulled his hand back and rubbed it dry on his jeans. "I'm doing fine. You don't have to worry about me. If I want to meet someone, I'll go try to meet them. Not everybody needs to dance to meet someone. Lots of women here are not dancing."

Barings waggled a finger at Albert. "Ahh, so you did come here to meet someone." He looked about the hall and his voice got higher. "Is it anybody I know, someone you met in town? Somebody special you'd hope to meet tonight?"

"Take it easy Barings or you'll have a heart attack. There's no actual person that I came to meet. I just wanted to see what the whole deal was."

"I knew it!" Barings cried, starting to dance a little jig and stabbing a finger into the air. "I knew it! I knew it! I knew it! Screw you Fency, I told you I was right. I just fucking knew it."

Albert backed away slightly. "What the hell are you talking about Barings? And why are you dancing like an idiot?"

"I told Fency that Harrison's dying got to you. I told him so, but he thought I was talking shit, man. But I was right, Albert. You just proved me right."

"What the hell's wrong with you, Barings? How can I prove you right if I have no idea what the hell you're talking about?"

"It's Harrison, man. Fucking Jerry Harrison. He got to you, didn't he? Jerry Harrison got to you."

"Jesus, Barings. Maybe you should stay off the dance floor and head right back to the Keweetan and sleep off whatever you need to sleep off," Albert said. "You're not making any sense."

"He got to me too, man. Fucking Harrison dying like that. Made me think about how sad that pathetic fucker was. And how there was no way I was going to end up like him. Even though I got his old job, I wasn't going to be like him. There's no way I'm going to die lonely like he did. No way. I'm going to meet some nice girl, Christ, even someone tonight and then we're going to get married and have a bunch of kids. And if Hydro ever decides to build that goddamn dam they keep talking about, I'm going to get a job with them and set me and my family up in a nice house."

"Jesus, Barings. Looks like you got you're whole life planned out."

"Not everything, just the important stuff," he said. "You gotta do that or you'll end up like Harrison. That's what his death taught me. If I figure things out a bit ahead of time, I won't end up like him."

"So how does all that make you right about me?"

"Because I figure Harrison's death hit you the same way. I told Fency that that's why you quit the Keweetan and settled here. You were looking to settle down. And when you said you were checking out the women that proved it to me that you don't want to end up like Jerry." Albert started to say something but Barings stopped him by waving a finger in his face. "And don't you tell me that I'm crazy because I know you pretty good Albert Apetagon and the look on your face tells me that I'm right. Right?"

Albert said nothing and glanced over Barings' shoulder. All around the room people were gathered along the walls or sitting at tables talking, smoking and drinking. They were all so engrossed in each other that they had not noticed Barings' crazy dance from a few minutes ago. Some of the people Albert knew by name and he knew they knew him. He didn't know some of the other people's actual names, but during the time he had spent working on the Keweetan and now in Jerry Harrison's old cabin — his cabin, he reminded himself — he had come to recognize their faces. Albert felt a smile growing on his face and he turned his focus back to Barings.

"Of course, I'm right." Barings playfully slapped Albert on the shoulder. "You're figuring out some kind of future for yourself just like me. And thank God too Albert, because we were getting all worried about it."

The smile disappeared. Albert narrowed his eyes at Barings. "Worried about what?"

"Shit, Albert. With you living in Jerry Harrison's old house, you're starting to get a reputation in town."

"Really? What kind of reputation?"

"I don't know, it's just people talking."

"And what are they talking about?" Albert growled.

Barings fidgeted uncomfortably. "I don't know. They see you quitting your job and taking over Harrison's house and traplines, just like that."

Albert shrugged and looked away. "Nobody seemed to want them. Why shouldn't I do what I did?"

"But you didn't ask anybody's permission or anything. You should have asked first."

"Who should I've asked, Barings? Jerry? He's dead. I found his body. You said so yourself, the man died sad, pathetic and lonely. He had no family, 'cause they're all dead or long gone, so who should I have asked? You tell me that."

"I don't know Albert, I'm just saying that you should have looked into things before you just took over Jerry's house and traplines. People started to talk."

"People can talk, I don't give a fucking damn."

"You're going to have to, Albert. You're not just some guy working on the Keweetan staying overnight on a Saturday anymore. You moving into Jerry's house and taking over his trapline now makes you a part of this town."

"So now I'm a respectable citizen of Grand Rapids. From the way you were going on before, I thought that would be a good thing."

Barings shook his head in exasperation. "There's no use talking to you Albert. You just don't get it. I can't seem to make you understand that things are different for you now."

"I know things are different for me know. I'm not stupid Barings, but I don't really care what some people are thinking or saying because I know what kind of people they are and we had the same kind of people like that in Norway House and they made no difference in my life."

Barings turned towards the dance floor, seeing the band climb back to the stage. He finished his drink and then placed an arm on Albert's shoulder. "I just wanted to let you know what's going on and that some people are worried. We didn't . . . " Barings trailed off, looking at the band gathering up their instruments to start another set. A group of guys and girls near the door waved at Barings. He waved back at them. There was a hum of feedback as the microphones were turned back on again. "Nobody wants you to turn into Jerry Harrison, Albert. Living all alone out there in that tiny house, people get worried that you'll become like him. That's what people are saying. They're worried that you are going to become just like Jerry."

Albert took a deep breath and stared at Barings for a long time. Even though the man could be annoying and placed value on things that didn't seem important, he did seem to care about Albert and what happened to him. Albert gripped Barings' hand and then gently removed it from his shoulder. "Don't worry Barings. I'm not going to turn out like Harrison. In my opinion he was a total waste of human skin."

Barings smiled brightly. "I knew that, Albert. And you proved it to me by checking out the women. Means you're thinking about the future." Barings turned and watched as the musicians gathered up their instruments in preparation for another set of music. "The band's about to start. You sure you don't want to come dance with us, Albert?"

Albert shook his head. "You go dance. I'll be fine."

"You're sure? It's loads of fun," Barings said with a wink. "And I can introduce you to some girls."

"Dancing's not my thing. I'll just hang out," Albert said, shaking his head. "And I don't need your help to find women, Barings."

"Your loss," Barings said. And he went back to the dance floor. Albert smiled and for several minutes watched the dancers and the band get everything started again. Soon the heat from all the moving bodies became too much so he stepped outside to get some air.

Outside of the dance hall, Albert leaned against the wall, sucking in the cool fresh air. He could still hear the music through the walls — the melody was muffled and the lower end of the bass sent soft vibrations through him — but more prominent were the chant of the crickets and the hum of the wind as it whispered through the leaves. There were smatterings of people all around him, groups of three, four or more, chatting quickly, laughing at some joke, or passing around a surreptitious bottle. A number of couples were also outside but they were more discreet, preferring to nuzzle and neck in the shadows. He was the lone single, disregarded by the couples, noticed yet ignored by the other groups. Albert sucked the clear air into his lungs, shut his eyes and thought about how he had gotten used to the new responses from people since finding Jerry Harrison's body and then taking over the dead man's cabin. When he was working on the Keweetan, he was Albert Apetagon from Norway House, a regular visitor to town because of the boat, an integral member in the chain of supply, so he was cordially greeted by the more permanent residents of Grand Rapids. Those few who knew some member of his family would always ask about that member of that family. But since he had given up his job on the Keweetan and become a de facto resident of town by moving into Jerry Harrison's old cabin and taking over his traplines, conversations would stop whenever he walked into the local Hudson Bay post, or when people would pass him on the street. No one would greet him, and those who knew members of his family no longer asked questions. If anybody offered any sort of greeting it would only be a slight nod.

He didn't mind the new reaction because for the first time in his life he was living alone, in his own place, taking care of his own needs. Barings and Barry Fency would visit once in awhile, telling him stories about the new guy Jacks or events that occurred during their runs around the lake. But they would always leave when it was time to go. He didn't have to share anything with anybody. Not unless he wanted. Albert figured that when it came time for him to share his new life, he would recognize it. Or it would recognize him.

A voice interrupted the crickets. "Albert," it said. And then a second later, it said it again, "Albert."

He opened his eyes.

Her face had a hint of native features, a slightly flattened nose, thin lips and thick dark eyebrows. But like many others in the town, she also had some northern European touches, light skin and bright blue eyes that looked so wide she seemed to be in a state of perpetual surprise. She must have been tall because she almost looked him in the eye. Her head was cocked to the side. "You're Albert Apetagon aren't you?"

He blinked quickly, his eyes surprised at this face standing so close to him. "What?" he said, barely getting the word out of his mouth.

Her face stretched out, every inch breaking out into a smile; a fragile glow, like a half moon on a cloudy night, wafted from her. "You're Albert Apetagon? You used to work on the Keweetan?"

Albert nodded. "Yeah. That's me."

She smiled again, breaking through the clouds. "That's what I figured. I saw you in the hall, standing in

the corner, talking to your friend, Wearings, or
something or other . . . "

"Barings," Albert quietly corrected her.

She shrugged. "Barings. Right. He's a supervisor or
the captain of the Keweetan, I'm guessing."

Albert chuckled. "He wishes."

"He's not in charge of the boat?" she asked, astonished. Albert shook his head. "He sure acts like he's the
big man on that boat. I danced a couple of numbers
with him and all you hear from him is how he had to
make this important decision in Riverton or how difficult it can be when there's a storm over the lake."

"Sounds like Barings."

"And your sure he's not the captain or somebody
important."

Albert shrugged. "He's important in some respects.
He's the crew chief, which means he oversees the
loading and unloading of the barges, and if you order
a barrel of kerosene, he'll make sure you get it."

"But he's not the captain?"

"Not even close."

"Well, he sure acts like the captain."

"He gets like that sometimes, but he's a good guy."

"Hmmm," she said with a nod, and then went silent.
She looked out into the woods, staring at the dark as if
she was mulling over what Albert said about Barings,
while Albert stared at her, wondering who this girl was,
asking himself if he had seen her before and had
forgotten her — though he doubted it— and studying
her, watching her lips part slightly as she breathed, how
she narrowed her eyes to focus on whatever she was
looking at in the forest and the way her brow crinkled

when a gust of wind rustled the trees. She quickly looked back at him, the shock of her blue-eyed gaze connecting with him so quickly and surprisingly that he jumped. He thought he may have even yelped — a few of the others around them seemed briefly startled — but she never reacted. She just stared at him, quizzically.

"You're the one who found Jerry Harrison," she said matter-of-factly. "I mean you found his body, right?"

Albert waited for a second, his memory quickly catching a glimpse of the grey pallor of Harrison's dead face. He was unsure of what to say in response to her question so he decided that a nod was fine.

She nodded back and a second later asked: "What was it like?"

Again, she surprised him. It was an obvious question but no one, not even Barings or Fency, had ever asked him that question about Harrison's body: "What was it like?" He quickly scanned her face, checking to see if she was messing with him, playing him like some sort of hermit fool that other people in the town had taken him for. But there was only curiosity and inquiry on her face. She really wanted to know what it was like to have found Jerry Harrison's dead body in the middle of his sad, pathetic cabin. Her question recalled the entire scene, even his imagining of Jerry's voice yelling at him from his eyeless face. The visions sent a shiver through his body, so deep that it didn't penetrate his skin and was invisible to anybody else. But it shook Albert to his core, dragged up all the thoughts of that terrible day and how sad Jerry Harrison's life had been. And it also reminded Albert that no matter what anybody else thought or what

Barings said that everybody else was saying about him, Albert Apetagon was no Jerry Harrison.

Albert looked back at this strange and familiar girl and told her the truth. "It was terrible."

She nodded once, accepting his simple explanation like it was a blessing from a priest. "That's what I thought," she replied.

After she stumbled for the third time, Albert reached out and offered his arm. She grabbed it, pulling him close, using him to balance her unsteady steps. "How can you see in this dark?" she asked. "I can't see a goddamned thing."

He smiled at her using the word goddamned. It sounded different coming from this woman, not angry like it did when his mother yelled the word and not wrong when kids said it to sound tough. "I can't see a thing either," he told her.

She clamped onto him tighter, attaching both her hands to his arm. "Then how the hell do you know which way you're going?"

"I've been using this path several times a day for the past eight months. If I don't know where I'm going by now, I'd be a pretty sorry excuse for a trapper."

"Do you really trap or is that just some sort of excuse for not working at a real job?" Something snapped, a branch or some leaves, and the girl shouted "Shit," and stumbled, almost falling out of Albert's grip. He quickly pulled her away from the offending tree, but said nothing in response to her predicament because he felt she deserved it for saying that trapping wasn't a real job.

"It's a real job all right. You wanna see the pelts? I got a few out there. Well at least the ones I'm going to use for myself. Most of them have already been sold to the Hudson Bay. I keep them in a little shed that I built next to the cabin. Jerry Harrison used to keep his pelts in the cabin with him. Saved on space but smelled the place up."

"They smell, don't they? Like rotten meat?"

"Not after you work them. But yeah, the ones I got smell. That's why I keep them in a shed, 'cause I don't want the smell in the cabin."

"I think I'll pass on seeing the pelts then." She moved closer to him, so close that he could feel some of her hair brush his neck, raising goosebumps in his skin. "Are we there yet?"

He pulled his arm out and draped it over her. She nestled into his shoulder. "Soon," he said. "Soon." He led her along the path through the dark forest, slowly down to guide her around ruts, roots or errant branches. The warmth of her body and the naturalness of how her shoulder fit into his chest made him silently forgive her for her remark about trapping. After several minutes, he pointed towards the clearing. "There," he said. "Just up ahead."

"What? I don't see anything."

"Just a few more steps and you will," he said, and led her into the clearing that held his cabin, his home. "This is it."

She held onto him for a few more seconds and then let go, stepping into the open area. She turned slowly, gazing in awe at the little clearing. It was an oasis of pale moonlight, like looking into the lake at dawn and watching the first breath of light reaching into the depths of the water, surrounded by high walls of dark trees. Stars which had been obscured by thick leaves, sparkled above, some of them seeming to move as invisible clouds drifted by. The soft tall grasses, almost unseen, like apparitions, wavered in the breeze.

"It's beautiful," she finally said, and Albert felt his chest swell. He knew it was beautiful. Fency and Barings had both told him that he had done a fine job of fixing the place up, but to hear this girl tell him that his home was beautiful gave him one of the happiest moments of his life. His skin seemed to hum with electricity.

"And my God, the cabin," she said, taking slow steps towards the structure. The cabin still sat in the middle of the clearing on a small rise. It was now bigger by a half, an addition hammered onto one end of Jerry Harrison's old place, and had been healed of its lean, standing up as if it grew straight out of the ground. And in the centre of each side wall there were windows, each divided into four panes of glass, offering a means to see in, out and through the cabin. "This couldn't have been Jerry Harrison's place. There's no way that old grouch lived in a place like this."

Albert followed to the cabin and tapped gently on the wall. "I fixed it up a bit," he said, trying not to sound too proud, but almost bursting. "Fency, one of the guys I used to work with on the Keweetan, helped out a bit. He smuggled some pieces of wood and other things to help."

She came over to him and hugged one arm around his waist. "It's beautiful," she said, smiling at him. They stared at each other for several seconds and then she asked, "Can I see the inside?"

"Of course," he said, with a quick nod. He guided her to the door.

"Where'd you get the door?" she asked, nudging him in the ribs. It was a heavy oak door, deep brown, the same colour as the doors on the Keweetan and with the same round windows that the boat's doors had.

"Like I said, I've got friends who help me out," he said, reaching for the knob. As he grabbed it and started to turn, she stopped him by grabbing his hands. He looked at her, perplexed. "You don't want to see the inside?"

She nodded, but her blue eyes stared at him. She had a look on her face, as if she wanted to ask him something but didn't know how to phrase the words. Finally she said, "Am I your first house guest?"

"Heck no," he said quickly, and he felt her hand grow cold and the light in her eyes extinguish at his answer. It took him a second to realize what her question really meant. "Barings and Fency visit me when they're in town. But they don't really count. Guess you're my first real house guest."

Her smile reached across the world and she turned his hand to open the door.

Some time later, as they lay in his bed glowing with sweat and catching their breath, Albert turned on his side and leaned on his elbow. He stared at her, wondering what the hell had just happened and why his cabin suddenly felt much bigger that it used to. He knew he had to ask her but wasn't sure how to approach the question. Finally he just blurted out the question: "What the hell is your name?"

There was a second and then she exploded into laughter. "You mean I never told you my name?"

He shook his head.

"God, I can't believe it. Didn't you ask me?"

Again he shook his head. "I couldn't find an opening, and by the time we got here it just never came up. So you going to tell me who you are?"

"Elaine," she said.

Albert stuck out his hand. "Nice to meet you, Elaine."

She looked at his hand, smiled at him and then shook it. "It's nice to meet you too, Albert."

GRAND RAPIDS

1

Sitting at a table in the Esso Restaurant, Albert slowly drifted out of his snooze to hear a set of light footsteps moving towards him. The scent of cooked meat drifted in, and a second or so later a mist of steam floated in front of his face. A plate clattered on the table in front of him and two warm hands gripped his shoulders. The hands kneaded his shoulders, his forearms and then slid down his chest. He reached up to grab them and opened his eyes. A glass of water and a plate of roast beef, mashed potatoes with gravy and mixed corn, carrots and peas sat in front of him. He took a deep breath and pulled the warm scent into his nose. His hands relaxed and Elaine, his wife for almost 40 years, stepped around him to sit on the opposite side of the table. She wore a black sweatshirt, a pair of faded jeans and a white apron covered with various restaurant stains. Elaine was a tall, stocky woman, almost equal in height to Albert and just a little less in weight. Unlike Albert, who seemed to carry his weight in his chest and stomach, Elaine's weight was more evenly distributed. But like Albert and many of the residents of the town, Elaine's face had a hint of native features mixed with European ones, but unlike many women her age, who fancied short tightly curled perms, Elaine's hair was straight and simply cut just above her shoulders. She looked at least ten years younger than her actual age.

She reached into the apron pocket and flicked a pack of cigarettes onto the table. She pulled it open, pulled out a cigarette and a lighter, and lit the cigarette. She blew the smoke off to the side, away from Albert and his meal.

"Nice special today," Albert said.

"Last day of the season," Elaine replied. "It's always roast beef on the last day of the season."

"We had chicken in the spring. At the end of the winter run."

"Chicken?" Elaine cocked her head to the side and gave him a questioning look. "Really?"

Albert took up his utensils and scooped some potatoes with his fork. "Uh-huh," he said, before sticking the food in his mouth.

Elaine shrugged. "Oh well, chicken, beef, whatever, it's always roast something on the last day of the season."

Albert cut a piece of meat and held it in front of his mouth. "Makes no real difference to me. It's always good . . . and cheap." He took the meat and chewed it. Then he added. "Like you."

Elaine slid back and slapped at him. Albert laughed and lifted his elbow; her hand, aimed at his head, cuffed him on the shoulder. "You!" she said. "I don't hear any complaints. Almost 40 years and not a complaint yet."

"Who's complaining," Albert said. "I was just speaking the truth."

"Well maybe I should start charging you."

"For the food?"

She swung at him again and he deflected the shot again with his shoulder. "The food's a deal you made with Keung. Anything else you had in mind, you have to deal with me."

Albert ate another slice of beef and another scoop of potatoes. "So what did you have in mind?"

"What do you mean?"

"If you're going to start charging me, I gotta know the price. So what did you have in mind?"

"I don't know. What's the going rate?"

"You're asking me? How the hell should I know? I'm a married man."

"So?"

"So when's the last time I was in Winnipeg? Last year?"

"Almost two years this October, when Bernie was in the hospital. Remember Billy stopped by and picked us up on his trip down from Norway House."

"So, you were with me," Albert said, pointing his fork at Elaine.

"Of course I was. Bernie was a close friend."

Albert dug into his food again. "So you're saying the last time I was in Winnipeg was with you, my wife, and we were visiting my brother's dying wife in the hospital."

Elaine nodded. "Right."

"Then how do you expect me to know the going rate when the last time I was in Winnipeg you were with me and we visited Bernie at the cancer clinic?"

Elaine pulled a long drag from the cigarette. "Why don't you ask your friend Sol?" she said while exhaling. "He knows."

Albert looked at her with a frown. "Sol doesn't know."

"Don't be so naive, Albert Apetagon," Elaine said. "Sol knows."

Albert set his utensils down and sat up straight. "How the hell would Sol know?"

"Why do you think he goes to Winnipeg every month?"

"His sister. He goes to visit his sister."

"Jackie gets on his nerves. And he gets on hers. Why would he visit her unless he has to?"

"Well, that's what he tells me."

"Of course he tells you that. You're his best friend. It's easier for him to tell you he's visiting his sister than telling you he's going to buy some company for the weekend."

"Maybe he's on band business. They've been doing a lot of work lately on the Hydro project."

"There's that, but what about the times he heads down alone. There's not that much band business going on in Winnipeg, even with the Hydro project."

"Jesus. Why the hell's he got to go to Winnipeg for, anyway?" Albert said loudly. "Shit, there's Norma Mason at the bar."

Elaine laughed. It was a full deep laugh, and like her voice, with a hint of gravel. Smoke from her cigarette was blown out with each laugh. "Norma Mason! You've got to be kidding. Sol Jacks and Norma Mason? What in hell would they have in common?"

"Who knows," Albert said, picking up his utensil and returning to his meal. "But she likes him, you can tell. Today when we went into the bar, she was all smiles around him saying 'Hi Sol. How you doing? How's the fishing?' and all that. She didn't even notice me until I said hi."

Elaine shook her head. "Norma Mason? Didn't Charlie just die?"

"Charlie Mason's been in the ground for more than three years. And before that he was in the hospital in Winnipeg for three months before cancer killed him." Albert cut and then placed a large piece of meat into his mouth. "Besides," he said while chewing, "Sol and Norma used to date before Charlie Mason came around and married her."

Elaine leaned forward. Her voice became a tight hiss. "Who told you that?"

"Sol did. In the bar today. Just after I told him that he and Norma should get together."

"You told Sol that he and Norma should get together?!"

"That's what I said. 'Sol,' I told him. 'I think Norma likes you. You two should get together and talk about old times.'"

"Albert Apetagon, I can't believe you said that to him," Elaine said with a smile. "What did Sol say about that?"

Albert chuckled. "He said I should go play my VLT and stay out of his games."

Elaine laughed, leaning back in her chair and shaking her head. "But Norma Mason? I don't think she's the right woman for Sol Jacks."

"Well she's probably better for him than driving six hours to Winnipeg every month and paying some woman to sleep with him," Albert said.

Elaine nodded slowly, but said nothing. She took a final drag from her cigarette and then stubbed the butt into the ashtray. She slowly stood up, blew a gust of air through her lips and placed a hand on Albert's shoulder. "I'll get you a coffee," she said, and headed towards the kitchen. Albert reached out, grabbed the back of her apron and slowly pulled. Elaine struggled slightly, giggled and then acquiesced, allowing herself to be pulled back. "Albert," she said. "Don't you want your coffee?"

"Just a sec," he said, reaching into his pocket, pulling out one of the red bills and handing it to her.

She examined the bill, incredulously turning it over and over. "Where'd you get this?"

He shrugged and resumed eating. "Old Jerry Johnson gave me some VLT advice and it paid off."

"Fifty dollars! That's some advice!" Her smile quickly became a frown. "You give him anything in return?"

"Wouldn't take it. Doesn't like to take responsibility for his advice."

"You should have given him something. Buy him a drink, whatever, but you should have given him something."

"I tried but he wouldn't take anything."

"You should have tried harder. We don't want everyone to think Albert Apetagon isn't thankful when someone helps him."

Albert raised his hands in defense. "I did try hard. I talked to that old goat for over five minutes trying to get him to take something for his trouble. Said we've been friends for 30 years and I would look bad if I didn't give him something in return, but he wasn't having any of it." Albert dropped his hands and turned back to his plate, stabbing a piece of meat with his fork. "Jerry Johnson's a crazy old geezer."

"He's not that much older than you."

"Yeah, but he looks and acts likes he's 80."

Elaine put her hand on Albert's shoulder. "Okay, so you tried hard. I'm sorry if I thought that you didn't." She felt the bill as if it wasn't real. "But why are you giving this to me?"

"If I kept it, I'd forget about it and it'd stay in my pocket for a couple weeks until you found it in the laundry all torn and useless. And you'd better put it away 'cause the kids are coming." Albert gestured with his head as his daughter Jessica, carrying her baby Melissa, came towards the station. Climbing out of their car and following behind her was her husband Brian and two of their kids, David and Samantha. The two adults saw Elaine and Albert and waved at them.

Elaine looked up and smiled. "Shit," she said, and then quickly tucked the bill into the front pocket of her jeans. "I'll get your coffee."

His daughter's family came into the restaurant. His granddaughter split from the family and headed to the kitchen. Samantha was a ten-year-old girl with straight hair that cascaded down to the small of her back, and like her mother and grandmother was taller than other girls her age. Elaine and Jessica stood five-ten, but Albert could see that Samantha would easily pass them and hit about six feet. She had the wide eyes of her grandmother and mother, the thin lips and soft chin of her father, and, fortunately, a slighter version of the Apetagon nose, the long thick knob of flesh that Albert had inherited from his father and that could be seen in photos of various Apetagons since the time the first camera ever appeared in Norway House.

The boy, David, headed into the back to grab a free coke and maybe some fries before he helped Lee Keung's son at the pumps. He gave Albert a wave as he did so Albert waved backed. In the looks department, David wasn't as lucky as his younger sister. He had the nose and all the Apetagon attributes. The pale brown skin, the thick mop of unruly black hair, the slight squint, the thick pucker in the upper lip, the tiny knob at the end of the chin and shoulders that almost grew directly from his head. Albert knew — not because everyone told him — that the boy was a direct reflection of him when he was thirteen. Everything about David, from the way he walked into a room, checking out every corner to see who was there, to the way his eyes stared almost unblinkingly through his squint while you talked to him. David's eyes, though, were green, inherited from Albert's mother. It was a colour that you didn't really notice at first because of the lowered eyelids, but once you did, they couldn't be ignored. Against the backdrop of the pale brown skin and the jet black hair, the eyes almost shone at you. You could even be talking to someone on the other side of the room, but if those eyes happened to be facing in your general direction, you'd find yourself drawn back to them.

"They're the devil's eyes," Lee Keung said one day while he, Albert and Sol Jacks watched David help Keung's grandson, Henry, pump gas, clean windshields and check the oil for Esso customers.

"What the hell does that mean?" Albert asked. "Devil's eyes?"

"That shade of green is the colour of the eyes of the devil."

"That some kind of Korean thing?" Sol asked.

"It's got nothing to do with Korea. It's a visual thing. All the art I've seen of the devil, even in the movies, show him with green eyes." He pointed out the window at David. "The same colour as David's, the eyes of the devil."

Albert shook his head at Keung. Christ, what a dumb thing for Keung to say, he thought. Next thing you know somebody would be saying that Lee Keung at the Esso thinks Albert Apetagon's grandson David is the devil. And then if he ever did anything bad, everybody would say that Keung knew what he was talking about: Apetagon's grandson is naturally a bad kid.

Keung saw the look on Albert's face. "What? I never said he was the devil, I just said David's eyes are the same colour as the devil's. David's a good kid. Hard worker too. He really helps us out."

For a second, Albert thought about stopping David from working at the Esso station, but he knew that David wasn't working at the gas station to help out Lee Keung; he liked hanging around with Henry Keung. The two boys were good friends and Albert didn't want to keep good friends apart because he knew what it meant to have good friends.

At the table, Albert's daughter Jessica and her husband Brian sat across from him. Jessica set the new baby down on her lap and then grabbed at the pack of smokes that Elaine had left behind. She pulled out her own lighter and blew the smoke in the air. Brian frowned at her. "You think you should be smoking? The kid's barely three months old."

Jessica took another puff, this time blowing the smoke directly into Brian's face. "You didn't have to carry the goddamned kid for nine months and give up drinking and smoking and coffee."

"I gave up all of that with you."

"You still drank beer though."

"Just a couple times a month. I don't think that counts."

"Of course it counts. You were supposed to quit with me for nine months and here you go out for a bunch of beers once a month."

"Oh come off it, Jess. It was only a couple beers."

"A couple's too many."

"And you didn't sneak any smokes in the bathroom?"

Jessica's face became indignant. "I did not!"

Brian laughed. "You did so. You don't think I knew what you were up to all those times sneaking off to the bathroom in the middle of the night."

"I was pregnant, you doofus. Pregnant women have to pee a lot."

"And since when does pregnant woman piss smell like cigarette smoke?"

"You followed me!"

"Just going pee myself. But it was like hanging 'round the bar with all the smoke in there."

Soon, Jessica and Brian's jammering became one big blur to Albert. They were an odd-looking couple, even for Grand Rapids. Jessica was an almost exact copy of her mother, a thick woman but with the height to make the thickness fit. Jessica always kept her hair in braids and normally wore jeans and a black T-shirt underneath a flannel shirt. And she'd always have another piece of clothing — a vest, a jacket, whatever, as long as it was made out of leather and covered in native beadwork. Jessica was heavily involved with the Band and felt she had to wear some type of native clothing to promote the image. Several of the elder women in town still practised the old crafts and Jessica always made sure she paid them top dollar for the work. But since the old women wouldn't accept the money outright — doing the work for another Band member wasn't something you charged for — Jessica just donated the money she would have paid to the Band and convinced Derby Johnston, the Band accountant, to add the money to the monthly cheque that went to all the elders.

Jessica's husband Brian, however, was as white as they come. Originally from Guelph, Ontario, he was an engineer who moved to Grand Rapids three years ago to help plan the upgrades to the dam. Brian wasn't as tall as Jessica but outweighed her by 50 pounds. Still, there wasn't an inch of fat on him. Underneath his suits and ties was a muscular body with broad shoulders and chest, thickly toned arms and thighs that were almost as thick as his waist. His face was rugged, with a chiseled jaw, a high broad forehead and behind his thick glasses were a pair of deep ocean-blue eyes. He had what Sol Jacks called "a geek brain trapped in a hockey player's body." As part of the planning for the dam upgrade, the provincial and federal governments were on Manitoba Hydro's case to deal with the local native community, and through the years Brian and Jessica met in meetings, and then they met alone after the meetings, at first to discuss certain parts of the project, and then late, for other reasons. A year ago, they married.

At first there was some controversy from all sides, business and personal. The Band was incensed at Jessica, and because she was marrying a white man, threatened to revoke her and her children's treaty numbers. It was an empty threat and she knew it, so they tried to fire her. But her position in the Band went deeper than just a job, so that too was an empty threat.

Hydro almost did fire Brian. He was just another engineer and there were plenty of those where he came from, but some member of the PR department thought the situation would play well. Even though he didn't like it, Brian became the unofficial poster boy for Hydro's new acceptance of native rights and culture. They weren't blatant about it; it was something they would mention in an offhand kind of way to other bands they were negotiating with, politicians they needed to placate or members of the media they needed to impress.

To Brian's parents, it didn't make any difference that Jessica was a highly respected member of the community and a member of the Band's negotiation team. They didn't care that she regularly met with corporate and government officials, or even knew the Minister of Indian Affairs, their own MP, on a first-name basis. She was just a conniving squaw to them, taking advantage of their lonely son so she could feed her kids. Brian tried many times to explain that she made just as much money as he did, but they didn't listen. And they both made several trips to Guelph to convince his parents otherwise, but they never got past the front door. Elaine even offered for her and Albert to drive to Guelph so the two sets of parents could talk and clear things up. "Forget it, Ma," Jessica had said. "They're the kind of people that if they saw two Indians on their front step, they'd call the police." Brian's parents were invited to the wedding, but didn't show up. Brian cut off all contact and they didn't even know about Melissa, their first grandchild.

Albert's feelings about Brian had nothing to do with whether he was Indian or not. It was his clothing. Brian was a nice guy and all, respectful to Albert, calling him first Sir, and then after an acceptable time Albert, but what bugged Albert the most was that Brian always wore dress pants and some type of dress shirt, even at small family gatherings. Sometimes, he even sported a jacket and tie. He didn't even own a pair of jeans, shorts, running shoes or workboots. It was unsettling because Brian made no effort to change his style of dress in order to fit in. Day after day, even on the weekends, he dressed like he was going to work at an office.

But when Albert saw how Brian instantly accepted Jessica's kids as his own, and continued to treat them as his own, he knew that the guy was all right. And when Brian and Jessica produced little Melissa, Brian became part of the family. His clothes made no difference any more, the strangeness of his dress began to wear off, and Albert got used to Brian's style, the same way he got used to his voice on the phone, or his laugh when he played with Jessica's kids.

"You hear about the IBA?" Jessica asked, snapping Albert out of his daze.

He didn't hear what she said, except for the word IBA. "What? What about the IBA?" he asked.

"Jesus, Dad, didn't Sol Jacks say anything about the IBA?" Jessica asked, frowning. "Man, I thought he'd be gloating about it all over town. Especially how he screwed Jack Dawson. Man, that was something. You should have seen it, it was a work of art."

"Oh that IBA," Albert said, taking a sip of lukewarm coffee to clear his head. "He said something about it, you know how Sol can go on about something, but I just sort of shut him out after awhile. He's probably telling everybody in the bar whatever story there is to tell, probably making stuff up, too, you know Sol. But I got out of there before he got started. After a few beers everything starts sounding the same from him. Gives me a headache."

"You going to tonight's meeting then?" Jessica asked.

"Might. Bud said he'd come by and pick me up, but I might just get to bed a little early tonight."

"You can't miss this meeting! It's probably the most important meeting in community history. You gotta make the meeting Pop."

"I'm still thinking about it. It all depends on how I feel later. Right now I'm pretty tired. It's been a long day."

Jessica started to say something more about the meeting but Brian sat up quickly, as if he remembered something important, and interrupted her. "Hey it's the last day of the season. Isn't that right, Albert?"

Albert nodded. "Yeah. That's why everybody's hanging around the bar. Last day."

"Good day on the lake?" Brian asked.

"Not bad," Albert said with a shrug. "Only four loads today. Pretty quiet."

"Season all right?"

Albert shrugged again. "Seen better years, but I've seen worse."

"You should forget about fishing, Dad," Jessica said, blowing cigarette smoke as she talked. "Going to be lots of jobs with this new IBA. Hydro's made some big promises that this time they'll have to keep."

"IBA only helps if you got a treaty number."

"Then get yourself a goddamned treaty number, Dad! I don't know how many times I got to tell you how important it is that you got a treaty number." Jessica stabbed out her cigarette, handed the baby over to Brian, and continued stabbing her finger at Albert. "There's a lot of money riding on the line, a heck of a lot of money and not just for Mom. If you got yourself a treaty number like the rest of us, you could buy yourself a new truck."

"Why does everybody want me to get a new truck?" Albert asked, but Jessica wasn't listening.

"Do you still have those forms I gave you months ago? Have you even filled them out or are they just sitting in some drawer? If you need help filling them out I can come over and help you."

Albert waved her away. "I don't need your help filling out the forms. I've just been busy."

"Well, you better not wait too long to fill them out. The IBA kicks in pretty fast. Better yet, I can fill them out for you and all you have to do is sign. That's what I should have done in the first place."

Albert felt himself fading out. Brian must have noticed because he shifted the baby in his arms and turned to Jessica. "Take it easy Jessica. Your dad's just had a hard day."

"I know that. I can see that he's had a hard day. But this thing is pretty important. He's got to fill out those forms — "

"And he probably will fill out those forms, when he gets the chance. Just let him rest and stop harassing him."

"I'm not harassing him," she said in a shocked tone. She turned to Albert. "I'm not harassing you am I Dad?" she asked him, but didn't wait for him to answer. "I just want to make sure you fill out your treaty forms in time — "

"There you go harassing him again," Brian said, thrusting the baby into Jessica's arms. "Give it a break, will you. Let the IBA thing rest for a bit."

Jessica's mouth opened wide in surprise. "I can't believe you said that. This IBA is the most important thing that's ever happened to the community. Why should we give it a rest? Huh? Why? 'Cause you Hydro guys now have to realize that there's a community of people here?"

"I didn't mean it like that. I just meant that you should lay off your father for a bit."

"Yeah, right. You're just saying that because you know I'm right. You Hydro guys don't like the IBA."

"What the hell are you talking about? Of course I like the IBA. It's about time Hydro got off its butt and made good for their mistakes."

"Sure you say that to me, but I bet that in the Hydro cafeteria it's a different thing. Probably complaining how us Indians are ruining your big upgrade project with all our stupid demands."

"Jesus, Jessie. What the hell's wrong with you? You know I wouldn't say anything like that."

"But you just did. You said I should give the IBA thing a rest."

"I was talking about your dad and your constant badgering of him."

Albert slid out of the booth with a deep sigh. The arguing had given him a headache. He walked towards the door of the cafeteria, searching for the fresh air and quiet of the outside. Jessica and Brian didn't try to stop him, but Jessica yelled after him, "You better come to the meeting Dad." Brian was instantly on her for harassing her father.

Albert continued walking, wondering how Jessica and Brian had become one of those bickering couples. They didn't get it from him and Elaine because they rarely fought. If Elaine didn't like something Albert did, she told him, not in a nasty voice, but so that he knew if he continued it would only make her more upset. If Elaine did something Albert didn't like, he wouldn't tell her but she could read his face and would keep asking him about it until he told her. Maybe it was because Jessica and Brian started their relationship on opposing sides and felt the need to keep up the image.

Albert walked out of the Esso station, across the parking lot. He looked left and right, checking for traffic, before he crossed the highway. He jogged slightly, just in case some hotrod came flying over the bridge.

His breathing was slightly laboured when he crossed the two lanes and started walking down the gravel road to his home. He heard someone call his name; it was faint, coming from across the road so he first thought it was his daughter and was about to ignore it. But the second time he heard it, it was someone else's voice, a male voice. He turned, searched for the location of the sound and found it. Fency's boy had just left the bar and was standing at the edge of the parking lot. He was facing Albert, holding up his right hand, fingers spread wide. Albert returned the gesture. Fency's boy held his hand up for another second, and then headed for home. Albert kept his hand up and watched as the boy dipped in and out of the ditch, dashed across the road and then jogged behind the Esso station where his bungalow was waiting for him. And probably Lee Keung's daughter, too. In a couple of weeks Irma Keung would head off to Winnipeg for university, and though Fency would resist it, he would follow her pretty quick. The boy was smart and knew what a good thing Irma was. Albert continued watching long after Fency had gone, thinking about how he would miss the boy when he left, and how, after two years, he still missed the boy's father.

Another voice called out, but closer: "Hey Grandpa."

Albert slowly turned and smiled at David's brilliant green eyes. The boy smiled back, bright and alive. Albert tousled David's hair. The boy put up a bit of a fuss, gently batting at his grandfather's hand, but didn't really mean it.

"What's up kid?" Albert asked.

David shrugged. "Not much."

"Hmmmm," replied Albert, and the two of them lapsed into a soft silence that neither felt the need to break. Albert stared at the lake, watching the clouds gather over the point where he had taken Barings' boat out that night two years ago. David also stared at the lake, with a quiet intent, like he knew what was out there, like he had spent as many years on the lake as his grandpa did.

After a few minutes of staring, Albert sighed. "You wanna walk me home?" he asked.

David shrugged again. "Sure. Why not?"

And then the two walked down the gravel road towards the trees and the roads that led to the northern part of the town. David wasn't yet as tall as Albert — he had another foot to go — but Albert walked slowly, almost strolling, so he had no trouble keeping up.

"How come you aren't at Keung's pumping gas with Henry?"

"I was getting bored," David said, drawing out the word bored into a long drawl. "Not enough cars coming through so it was pretty slow."

"So you decided to come hang out with your old grandpa, eh? 'Cause you were bored?" Albert's voice was playful as he too drew out bored into a drawl.

"No, that's not it," David said with an indignant tone. "I just saw you standing there looking out at the lake. You didn't move for a long time so I figured I'd come see what you were looking at."

"I was looking at the lake," Albert said.

"That's what I figured." David kicked at a rock, driving it into the ditch. "See anything interesting?"

It was Albert's turn to shrug. "Not much. Just a lot of water."

"Talk about boooorrring," replied David, and he jumped away just as Albert took a swipe at his head. David danced around a bit and Albert swiped at him a couple more times, but then they resumed their normal pace down the road, taking the 90-degree turn and walking the half a kilometre to the road that led to Albert's house. They said nothing until they reached the driveway to Albert's trailer. His old green truck sat useless in the yard, surrounded by bits of fishing gear, pieces of white styrofoam coolers, a couple of rust-red animal traps, some engine parts, old cardboard boxes, a swing set that leaned to the left and had only one swing, three and a half lime-green lawn chairs, various pieces of wood, some green bags of trash that hadn't yet been collected, old cans and bottles and a number of other things, the flotsam and jetsam that sat in pretty much everybody's yard in this part of Grand Rapids.

Albert walked into the yard, but David didn't follow him. He stood at the threshold, as if he were waiting for something. It took Albert several steps to realize that David wasn't with him any longer. He turned and saw him staring at the old green truck as if he was in some kind of trance.

"You wanna come in for a bit?" he asked. "I got some Kool-Aid or some other kind of coloured water for ya. You could probably watch some TV if you want. I know your mother doesn't let you watch the violent stuff, but I bet we could find us some wrestling somewhere on the dish. There's always gotta be some sort of wrestling going on somewhere."

David shrugged and it took him so long to speak, that to Albert, the boy seemed to disappear. And when he did speak, it was so quiet that Albert didn't hear at first and had to move closer. Albert knew David had asked him a question but he wasn't sure what the question was.

"Sorry David, I didn't hear you."

David cleared his throat and asked his question a little bit louder. "You going fishing tomorrow?"

Albert was about to respond with a no, and had even started to shake his head, but stopped himself when he realized what David was really asking him. "You want to come along?" Albert asked tentatively.

David nodded, but shrugged at the same time. "If that's all right. If not, that's okay."

"Well today was the last day of the season so I wasn't planning to go out," Albert started, feeling the arthritis twinge in his fingers and his shoulders. But he saw David deflate for a brief second. The boy managed to catch his disappointment and shrug it off, but it was enough for Albert to see. He started to turn to walk away.

"That's okay, Grandpa. Yeah, I forgot today was the last day. Maybe later, okay?"

Albert shook off the arthritis, or at least tried to. David couldn't start fishing till he was sixteen, but three years wasn't that long of a time. "Well shit, so what if today was the last day? Doesn't mean we still can't go out on the lake and catch some fish," Albert said, enthusiastically. "We just won't sell them to Barings that's all. And whatever we catch we can stick 'em in the freezer or throw 'em back if we get too many. How's that sound?"

David turned, trying to temper his excitement with a simple shrug of his shoulders, but his face still glowed with happiness. "That'd be cool Grandpa," he said with only a slight bit of enthusiasm in his voice. "You sure you won't get into trouble?"

Albert smiled, thinking about how two years ago Barry Fency had asked him the exact same thing from his hospital bed: "You sure you won't get into trouble, Albert?" Fency's voice was barely there, like a line cast upon the lake, when he asked the question.

Albert answered his grandson with the exact same words he said to Barry Fency that night two years ago. "Who cares? Some things are more important," he said. And then, to David, he added, "but we gotta be on the lake pretty early so you gotta be up by three and over at my boat by four. If you're not there, I'm leaving without you."

David nodded quickly, giving a thumbs up. "Right. Up at three. At your boat by four. You got it."

Albert slapped David on the shoulder. "Good. And dress warm, with boots and gloves, 'cause it's pretty cold out there in the morning. If you need anything, I can probably lend it to ya."

David pointed at Albert's coveralls. "You got any of those for me?"

Albert tugged at his coveralls. "These won't fit you, but maybe I got some old ones lying around. They used to belong to Mr. Fency, he was a small guy, a little bit bigger than you, but they might fit. You never know. Your grandmother was sewing them up for him, but didn't get them back to him before he died. That all right with you, wearing Fency's coveralls?"

"Okay with me, I guess," David said. His voice was unsure. "Is it okay with you, having me wear them?"

"Well, somebody ought to use them. I'll dig them out of the closet and bring a set down for you tomorrow morning. If they don't fit, then we'll just stick them in the bottom of the boat." Albert reached into his pocket and pulled out the other red bill that he had won at the VLTs. David's eyes bugged out at the bill. Albert handed to him and David tentatively took it, holding it between his thumb and forefinger like it was a delicate flower.

"That's not for you," Albert said sternly. "I need you to run some errands for me. You got time?" David nodded, so Albert continued. "Okay. Head down to Keung's and tell him that Albert needs a couple hundred yards of line and a couple of cans of gas for my engine and about five coolers and ice packs for the fish. Don't show him that bill until he tells you how much it's going to cost, and then tell him to give you Albert's regular price. You got that? Make sure you tell him that this order is coming directly from me and I want my regular price, got that?"

David nodded. "Couple hundred yards of line, gas, coolers, ice packs and Albert's regular price."

"Right. Then go over to your grandma on the restaurant side and tell her that we're going to need two lunches 'cause you and me are going on the lake tomorrow. She probably won't ask, but if she does, just tell her you and I are going fishing. Tell her you asked me to teach you how to fish, but only if she asks. If she doesn't, don't bother. There's no need to wait for the food because she'll bring it home here. If you want her to make you something special, ask her, but don't expect Christmas turkey. Just pick the sandwiches you like, all right?"

David nodded, so Albert continued. "Okay, and then when you're done there, take all the gear Keung gave you and take it over to my boat. Fill up the tank and put all the rest on the bottom. Tuck the coolers upside down and under the seats because it's probably going to rain tonight and put the line under them. I don't want stuff blowing away in the wind. You got that?"

"Sure Grandpa, fill the tank and put the rest of the stuff in the boat so it doesn't blow away. Is that it?"

Albert laughed and slapped David on the shoulder. "For today that's it. Tomorrow's a different story. Well, don't stand around here." Albert clapped his hands. "Chop chop. It's going to be a long day tomorrow and you've got work to do before you go to bed."

"Right Grandpa," David said, and started running towards town. "I'll see you tomorrow!" he shouted.

"Be at my boat at four! And don't be late!" Albert shouted back. David responded with a wave.

Albert watched the boy run down the road and disappear around the corner towards town. Albert turned and went into his trailer, thinking about how he could keep his license long enough so he could pass it on to David. Three years wasn't that long of a time, he thought. He could keep his license as long as he fished at least one season of the year, and he didn't really have to fish the whole season, just part of it. If he wanted, he could miss winter and spend the cold months warm in his trailer while Sol and Abe and Barings' boys huddled in their parkas, drilling holes through the thick ice. Maybe there was a cushy job at the dam, or better yet, he could finally get his treaty number and with the IBA money everybody was talking about he could take it easy

and hang out with Jerry Johnson at the bar in the after-
noons, popping quarters and loonies into the VLTs,
hoping for a succession of straights to make the day
seem a bit brighter.

There was a slight smell of mould and stale air inside
Albert's trailer. The front door led directly into the
kitchen. The room was not the most luxurious in the
world: the cupboards were shit brown in colour, the
appliances were at least fifteen years old, the fridge
chugging away like a mufflerless pickup, the linoleum
cracked and buckled in several places and the window
over the sink a layer of dust on the inside of the glass.
But to Albert the room was cozy. It looked like people
actually lived there on a daily basis, and besides, the
room was a pretty good size for a trailer, enough room
to put a formica table with four matching chairs in the
centre of the room. The table still had dishes from his
and Elaine's separate breakfasts. She never got up when
he did during a season, so Albert gathered up the dishes
and cutlery and stacked them on the counter by the
sink. There was a stack of clean dishes sitting in the sink.
Elaine must have left them to dry, and Albert rummaged
through them, looking for a tall glass. He found one and
stepped over to the fridge, opening it and pulling out a
pitcher of red Kool-Aid. He poured himself a glass and
put the pitcher back into the fridge, shutting the door
behind him. Albert took a sip of the sweet liquid and
walked into his living room. David might not like fishing,
he thought, but then again, he might. Maybe the boy
might like fishing at first, then discover girls and forget
about getting up at three in the morning. Teenagers
were like that, they liked to sleep as long as possible, and

David was just a year or two away from that. He might think it's cool to fish now. Next year, who knows.

Albert sat down on his Lazee Boy, the leather peeling off the arms of the chair and the springs groaning under his weight. The big chair was off to the side of the long living room, facing the picture window and the TV. There were also a love seat and chesterfield in the room, a matching set in a bright floral print facing each other on opposite sides of Albert's chair. There was a heavy dark box of a coffee table in front of the couch and two end tables on opposite sides of the love seat. The coffee table was covered with newspaper, magazines, Elaine's knitting and circular water stains, and every inch of the end tables was covered with frames holding photos of various children, grandchildren and great-grandchildren.

The blinds over the picture window were closed, but the sun from the west bathed the room in a soft yellow glow. Albert took another drink from his glass and set it down on the floor next to him. He thought about turning on the TV, but passed on the idea. He figured that after a bit of a sit, he'd take off his overalls and the rest and take a hot shower to clean the lake off of him. He thought about that for awhile, and thought about what he would teach David tomorrow out on the lake. At the very least, he could do that: teach the boy how to fish, how to string a line out into the water, how to watch the shifting colours to search for the fish, and how the reflection of the water in the low dark clouds could point the way to 25 cartons of fish. David would learn everything Albert could teach him and he wouldn't have to wear sunglasses and use all the fancy gear. But if he wanted to, that would be fine with Albert, as long as he wanted to be on the lake.

But then again, next year, or whenever, David might not want to fish like his grandpa, but at the very least Albert would show him how it was done. What he did with it after that,was up to him. Albert couldn't make him fish; he could only teach him how.

Albert felt a little lighter after that, grabbed his glass and drank the rest in one gulp. He set the empty glass back on the floor and decided it was now time to get up, time to get rid of his clothes and shower the smell of fish, sweat and the lake off of him. But the chair felt so comfortable around him — his arthritis had quieted — so before he even managed to think about showering again, he drifted off, dreaming about that night on the lake.

TWO YEARS AGO

Fency's boy steered the boat towards the lake. The company boat pushed through the darkness, slicing an invisible line through the black surface. The lights of the town disappeared once they rounded the point, but there were a few scattered lights along the shore to the northwest. There had been a brief screech from the shore just as they came around the point, some bird, likely an owl, plucking a rodent from the ground for a meal, but after that their only companions in sound were the whine of the engine and the slapping wash of the water against the side of the boat.

Albert tried to keep himself busy by first rolling up the ropes and stacking them neatly below the gunnel. Next, he took a few of the lead weights that helped drop the fishing lines into the lake and tied them to the body, fastening the rope around the ankles. Finished, he returned to a seat near the stern and sat down. Fency's boy stood at the wheel driving the boat, and Albert watched him for several seconds. The boy stood stiff and straight, his face unbending against the wind, doing his best to ignore the body of his father lying on the deck behind him. Albert couldn't bring himself to look at the body either, so he looked up. The Milky Way stretched before him and a minuscule dot of light drifted across the sky. Albert watched the satellite travel across the backdrop of stars and then lost it when he blinked. He

248

searched the sky but was unable to find the satellite again.

Some time later, the engine stopped and the boat drifted forward on the momentum. The silence of the lake, previously stolen by the sound of the engine, returned. Water lapped against the sides of the boats and a slight breeze whistled in the air. Fency's boy pulled a pack of smokes from his pocket and lit one. He took several deep puffs and turned around. Albert stood up and moved to drop the anchor. "Leave it," said the boy. "We're not going be here long." Albert stood at ease, and for a few seconds they stood in silence, staring out at the lake, each in a different direction. Finally, Albert sighed. "Let's get this thing over with then."

Albert and Fency's boy reacted simultaneously, stepping forward and grabbing opposite ends of the blanket. Albert held the feet and the lead weight; the boy held the head and the upper body. They carried the body to the port side and balanced it on the gunnel, each resting a hand on the body to hold it in place.

Albert looked at the boy, but he was staring out at the lake, averting his gaze from the body. Albert took a deep breath and then spoke. "I met Barry Fency when I started working loading and unloading supplies on the Keweetan on its week-long run around the lake. I was only seventeen years old and I moved from Norway House because I didn't feel like working on the railroad anymore. The three of us — Barings, Fency and Apetagon — worked together for two years on that boat with Jerry Harrison, our crew chief, screaming blue murder at us all the time. I almost quit once because of all that screaming, but your dad talked me out of it. He said that Harrison was just a sad old fucker with no family and no friends and the only way he could relate to anyone was either to cower like some pup to a wolf or to yell at them like a magpie. He said that anytime Harrison's yelling got to me, I should picture him in his pathetic, puny cabin sitting all by himself. After that, Harrison never really bothered me anymore.

"After Elaine and I got married and I got a boat to do some fishing, your dad decided to quit the Keweetan and follow me out. We fished on that lake for about ten years, and then they decided to build the dam, so we got jobs doing that. And then when the dam was done, we headed back out onto the lake and started fishing again. But then he got cancer." The words got caught in Albert's throat. He tried to shake and blink the tears away but they drifted down his face. He looked up from the body and saw the boy looking at him, a stream of tears below each eye. When their eyes met, Fency nodded, giving Albert the strength to continue. "We didn't do anything real important but we caught a lot of fish. Your dad used to say you got to live a certain time and if you didn't do anything to change the world that was fine as long as you did something you liked to do." Albert went silent for a few seconds, staring out at the lake looking for something only he could see.

"I'm done so if you want to say something, you go ahead," Albert said.

Fency's boy shook his head slowly. "He knows what I'd say so there's no point in saying it."

"Give me a puff of that smoke, will you?" Albert said. The boy nodded and with his free hand he handed it over. Albert took a drag from the smoke and offered it back but it was declined. Albert puffed once again and then put the cigarette into the mouth of Barry Fency. A second later, the ember glowed brightly. A thin sound escaped from Barry's lips as he puffed on the cigarette. Albert left the cigarette in the mouth, nodded once and then lifted his hand from the body. The boy immediately followed. Barry Fency balanced on the gunnel for a second and then fell into the water. There was a splash, several whitecapped ripples, and the body slipped into the black lake. The ripples dissipated quickly, leaving no evidence of the body's acceptance.

Albert stared at the spot for several seconds, listening to the waves. As they lapped against the boat, they seemed to be speaking to him, a soft murmur. Finally, he took a deep breath. "Let's head back in," he said. Fency's boy stood up and went to the front of the boat. Seconds later the engine roared to life, once again stealing the silence of the lake.

An instant later, the incessant honking from a horn jerked Albert out of his dream. "Barry," he muttered, and for a second he thought he was still on the lake. But the low sunlight through the trees showed him where he was. He blinked several times and realized that it was Bud making all the racket.

Albert checked his watch for the time and saw that he had been out for almost three hours. Outside the trailer, Bud was alternating between yelling for Albert and honking his truck's horn.

"Hey Albert!" Beep Beep!

"Wake up!" Beep! Beep! Beep!

"Let's get a move on!" Beeeeeeep!

"All right! I'm coming!" Albert shouted. "Keep your shorts on!"

"The meeting's going to start pretty quick!" Bud shouted back, giving one last push on his horn.

"Yeah, yeah. The meeting," Albert said to himself. The voice of the lake still spoke to him from the dream. It was comforting, a greeting from an old friend. But mixed in with the sound was the voice of Barry Fency, saying the same phrase over and over. That night on the lake, Fency had whispered one last statement before dropping into the water. "See ya, Albert," was all he said. And sometimes, when Albert drifted his boat into the shore after a day of fishing, he would hear his friends' voices, saying goodbye but inviting him to return when he could.

Maybe it would be his final season, maybe it wouldn't. It was too early to tell. He'd decide later, after the meeting. After tomorrow's fishing with David. After . . .

Bud honked again, this time demanding action.

Albert sighed deeply and pushed himself out of his comfortable chair.